THE WEB OF WAR

Claire Grant, a radar operator in the WAAF, still mourning the death of her parents and brother in an air raid, finds coming on leave to her grandmother's home difficult to face. Martin, a friend from her school days, now a pilot in the RAF, helps her to come to terms with her grief and encourages the flimsy rapport between Claire and her grandmother. War rules their lives and it is some time before they meet again. Claire is in love, but there are many quirks of fate yet to be faced.

Books by Hilary Grenville
Published by The House of Ulverscroft:

APPOINTMENT IN VENICE
THE TOLMAR TRUST
HERITAGE OF DEATH

Class No. _____ F _____ Acc No. C/81494

Author: GRENVILLE, H   Loc: _____

LEABHARLANN
CHONDAE AN CHABHAIN

1.

2.   weeks. It is to be
                                             te stamped below.
                                             for every week or

F / C81494

GRENVILLE, Hilary

HILARY GRENVILLE

THE WEB OF WAR

Complete and Unabridged

ULVERSCROFT
Leicester

First Large Print Edition
published 1999

British Library CIP Data

Grenville, Hilary
    The web of war.—Large print ed.—
    Ulverscroft large print series: romance
    1. Love stories
    2. Large type books
    I. Title
    823.9'14 [F]

    ISBN 0–7089–4048–X

Published by
F. A. Thorpe (Publishing) Ltd.
Anstey, Leicestershire
Set by Words & Graphics Ltd.
Anstey, Leicestershire
Printed and bound in Great Britain by
T. J. International Ltd., Padstow, Cornwall

This book is printed on acid-free paper

1

The crowded compartment darkened. The black rock face towered above the slowing train and through the open window came the unmistakable whiff of Lime Street: the mingling of soot and steam and stale Liverpool air.

It was a Friday afternoon in the spring of 1943. Since nine that morning Claire Grant had been travelling from a remote RAF Station in Yorkshire at the start of ten days' leave.

In the past, coming into Lime Street Station had meant coming home to the tall Edwardian house overlooking the estuary of the River Mersey. The acrid smell wafting through the open window evoked those memories so strongly that Claire found herself almost believing the impossible. But that momentary frisson of excitement was a mockery. Home, once so solid and welcoming, no longer existed. Two years and four months had gone by since a direct hit had reduced the house to a pile of rubble, killing her parents and her young brother, Peter. Claire had been seventeen at the time:

1

old enough to resist being treated as a child; young enough to need her parents more than at any other time in her life.

The train jolted and moved into the station. Kit bags and suitcases were hauled from the racks. For some, the numbing boredom of the journey was giving way to excited anticipation, but not for Claire. She was going to stay with her grandmother, for whom Peter had been the favourite, and Claire felt guilty for being the survivor. Neither she nor her grandmother had yet come to terms with their grief. Now, in the midst of all the activity of arrival, Claire felt isolated. Alone.

Carried along with the solid mass of passengers and luggage, she stepped onto the platform and threaded her way towards the barrier. Showing her travel warrant, she turned to join the taxi queue.

'Carry your bag, Miss?'

For a moment she failed to recognize the tall Air Force officer who took the holdall from her hand.

Martin Turner, the boy next door, was no longer the lanky schoolboy of their last meeting. The change was too much to take all at once. He was still lean, but broader in the shoulders, his manner altogether more assured. The welcoming grin no longer stretched from ear to ear, but there was the same sparkle of fun in the brown eyes.

'Martin! Fancy bumping into you. Did you come off this train?' She looked around. 'Or, are you meeting someone?'

'I'm meeting you, you idiot.'

'How did you know I was coming on leave?'

She stood back, feeling suddenly and absurdly shy. Even before the bombing they had lost touch, with Martin away at school and later going briefly to university before volunteering for the RAF. Small wonder they were like strangers.

'I went to see your grandmother,' he said. 'She told me you'd be arriving this afternoon. I thought it was time we got re-acquainted.'

She touched the wings on his tunic. 'You made it. Good for you.'

He shrugged. 'They're handed out with the rations.'

The corners of her mouth puckered in amusement at the uncharacteristic modesty.

'What are you flying? Spitfires?'

He shook his head, and she thought she could detect a tinge of regret in his reply. 'Wimpeys . . . Wellingtons. I'm stationed not far from Oxford.'

He glanced at the growing queue. 'Shall I

persuade a taxi driver to take us through the tunnel?' he said. 'It's probably the quickest way.'

Claire was in no rush to get to her grandmother's house. 'No. I hate queues,' she said, making that her excuse. 'Let's get a tram down to the ferry.'

The clatter of the busy procession of tram-cars reinforced that impression of Liverpool which Claire had never felt quite so potently before. Martin pushed her ahead of him aboard the first one clanging to a stop near the centre of the road. The conductor tugged the overhead cord, called out, 'Hold tight!' in a thick Liverpool twang, and the bell jangled twice. The driver swung the brass handle in front of him and they were off, jogging and rattling along the rails, turning down the hill towards the river.

'What's wrong, Claire?' Martin said. 'You look bothered. You still feel they ought to be there, waiting for you. Is that it?'

'Perhaps.'

'Believe me, I do know what you're going through. I've been there too.'

She looked puzzled for a moment, and then she said, 'Of course . . . before the war . . . when your mother died. I could only guess what you were going through then. It was unknown territory. I couldn't have been much help to you.'

'You listened while I let off steam. That's what I needed. But that was a long time ago. It may seem like an endless, dark tunnel, but you do come out at the other end, I promise you.'

She was silent for while, concentrating on the view from the window: the burnt-out department stores — gaps like missing teeth in an old mouth; small shops with boarded-up windows, and signs proudly boasting, 'Business as usual'.

They had reached the terminus — the nest of trams parked in front of the Liver Building, that ultimate distinguishing mark of the city — before she spoke again.

'I've been dreading this leave,' she admitted, as they followed the other passengers towards the landing stage. 'Back at camp there are so many other things to think about. Here, I get submerged in the past. I've got ten days. And you?'

'I'm due back tomorrow,' he said.

She felt as though a lifeline had been whisked away.

They half walked, half ran down the slipway made steep by the low tide, to where the ferry boat waited at the landing stage. Climbing to the upper deck they sat on a wooden seat by the rail, looking out over the river. Claire took off her cap, shaking her head and letting the breeze ruffle her hair, pale gold in the late afternoon sunshine.

The gangway was hauled ashore. The water churned and the boat began to manoeuvre across the river, avoiding the superstructure of the wrecks just breaking the surface — another legacy of the air raids.

'What made you join up?' Martin asked.

'You sound as though you disapprove.'

'I do.'

'You'd prefer to think of me sitting at home knitting Balaclava helmets, I suppose?' she said dryly.

He laughed out loud. 'You sounded exactly like your grandmother then.'

'Well, in that case, I got away not a moment too soon.'

'Oh, come on! You don't mean that.'

'But I do,' Claire insisted. 'She's as hard as granite. I don't want to end up like that. I'll admit she's been good to me, but there's no warmth there. Peter was always her favourite. You know that as well as I do. I can't help feeling that she must resent the fact that he's gone, and I'm still here.'

'You're wrong,' he said angrily. 'Naturally, she's sad that Peter is dead. So are we all. Can't you understand? Like you, she needs time to adjust. And, don't forget, *she* hasn't been able to get away from all the reminders.'

Claire was shaken by his outburst, expecting support, not criticism. The impact of his words stirred up anger and resentment, but also forced her to reconsider her own attitude.

The truth dawned slowly.

'Martin . . . what a fool I've been. I must have been in blinkers. For Grandmother, it's all happened before. Perhaps that's why she's always seemed so thick-skinned. I wish I'd known my grandfather. He was killed in France in 1916, only a few months after Uncle James.'

'James? Was he your father's brother?'

She nodded. 'He died of wounds at Verdun.'

'Her husband, her two sons, her grandson, and your mother. No wonder she's grown a defensive shell. I'm more convinced than ever that you should have stayed at home. She's not the tough old bird she was, you know. She's changed a lot since I last saw her.'

'At least *she* understands why I joined up — why I had to go. I can't hide behind her skirts. I wouldn't want to, and she'd hate it. And, you're forgetting, she's got Blodwen to care for her.'

'Blodwen's not family.'

'Rubbish!' It was Claire's turn to be annoyed. 'She's been part of the family since she came from Wales as a 'mother's help' when Daddy was a small boy. They're devoted to each other.'

She got up, leaning on the rail, gazing at the opposite shore, following the line of the promenade towards the estuary mouth.

Martin stood beside her.

'You can't see it from here,' he said, knowing that she couldn't help looking towards the ruins of her old home, one of the many holes in the landscape. He put a comforting arm around her shoulders. 'Don't keep on fighting it, Claire. It's happened. Life has to go on.'

'But, nothing will ever be the same again.'

'Not for you . . . not for me . . . not for countless thousands like us,' he agreed. 'But was it so perfect? Don't forget the dole queues; the children without any shoes.'

Her eyes were bright with tears. 'It's a hell of a price to pay to cure unemployment!'

'Claire! I didn't mean to upset you. Don't let's quarrel. Life's too . . . ' He stopped abruptly.

'Yes. Much too short,' she said, completing the sentence for him.

Immediately, she regretted the words. Who

would know better than he that life was precarious?

She looked up at him apologetically. 'Sorry, Martin. A stupid thing to say. I'm not a child any more. I ought to be able to cope.'

'You've kept it all locked away inside you for too long,' he said. 'It's got to come to the surface sometime.'

'Not so easy with Grandmother.'

'Stiff upper lip, and all that?' He had a way of mixing sympathy with teasing which she found easier to accept. 'You can talk to me,' he said. 'I'm a good listener.'

The boat nudged the landing stage and, just as they had done when they were children, they hurried down the companionway, stamping on the gangway as it touched the deck, and stepping out ahead of the crowd. They laughed in the knowledge that they had slipped back in time, finding each other in the familiarity of old-established ritual.

The buses were lined up at one side of the road. The top deck of the number sixteen was empty.

'Were you taken to hospital after the bombing?' Martin asked as the bus pulled away.

Claire knew he was doing his best to make her loosen up and talk about it. But she was tense again, afraid to remember.

'I was in the RAF by then,' Martin said, 'learning to fly, in Canada. Father waited to tell me what had happened in that raid until I was back in this country. I was coming home on leave and he suggested that we should meet at the cottage in North Wales, but we ended up at The Grosvenor in Chester. The old man likes his creature comforts. It was a hell of a shock. I was angry that I hadn't been told earlier, and I wanted to get in touch with you, but he told me you'd been sent away to finish your exams.'

'Yes. The school had been bombed, and Grandmother was determined that I'd get my Higher Certificate.'

'Father couldn't describe the raid because he'd been in London at the time. I don't think he's ever forgiven himself for not being there when you needed him, but he had to be in London that weekend. It must have been hell. No wonder you're all screwed up. Give it an airing, Claire. Tell me about it.'

She was silent for a while, and then she said hesitantly, 'It had never been so concentrated before . . . so pulverizing. It was the first time I'd been really scared. We'd been playing Snap under the stairs.' The ghost of a smile relaxed the taut muscles of her face. 'Peter had been cheating, as usual.'

The smile faded. 'I don't remember hearing the bomb that hit us. I don't remember any explosion. That's my only comfort.' She glanced up at Martin and knew he understood. 'The rescue squad must have arrived soon after I regained consciousness. I was trapped, unable to move, and the fire was getting a hold by then.'

With every sentence she was reliving the horrors of that night.

Again she fell silent, and Martin, hoping he had not pushed her too far, waited for her to continue.

'One of the doors had been thrown across the hall by the blast,' she went on. 'It saved my life. It was like a sloping roof over my head, holding back the wreckage. But, the door kept moving. Every time it happened they had to stop. I could hear the rubble shifting. The smoke and the dust filled my lungs until I could hardly breath, and the heat from the fire came at me in great waves. I thought they'd never get me out. I was convinced that I was going to be crushed, or . . . burnt alive.'

'I can understand why Father hates himself for not being there to support you.'

'He shouldn't feel guilty,' Claire insisted. 'He couldn't have done anything if he'd been at home. The rescue squad knew exactly what they were doing. They wouldn't allow anyone else to help. One false move would have had the whole lot on top of me.'

She shivered.

'Don't force it, Claire. Telling someone can take the pressure off, but the time has to be right.'

'There's not much more to tell,' she said. 'They got me out just before the whole lot collapsed. There was an ambulance there to take me to the hospital. When I was carried into the crowded ward I couldn't speak, just lay there like a dummy while they cleaned me up and put on a few dressings. Shock, I suppose. My clothes were in shreds and singed by the fire. There was blood everywhere, but I wasn't badly hurt.'

'And your grandmother picked you up?'

She nodded. 'One of the rescue squad got her address from someone in the road. Even when I saw her, I didn't really grasp what had happened. I suppose it sounds stupid, but it was all so unreal, like a nightmare I couldn't quite latch on to, or escape. In all the hell of that morning, Grandmother walked down the ward, beautifully groomed, looking just like a fashion plate.'

'That doesn't surprise me,' he said. 'She must have been stunning when she was younger. She's a remarkable woman.'

'She's that, all right.' Claire paused. 'It was just before Christmas, and she wouldn't ignore that, whatever else happened. Looking back, I'm convinced she made a special effort to make things seem as normal as possible.'

Although Claire had been unable to give Martin the full picture of the horrors of that night, she experienced a tremendous sense of relief. By the time they drew near to her grandmother's house, she became aware that she no longer dreaded the next ten days.

'Blodwen's waiting at the gate,' Martin said, and they both waved to the dumpy figure as they quickened their pace.

'Claire, fach!' Blodwen hugged her and then stood back. 'You look a bit thin. Feeding you all right, are they?'

Assuring her that she was not being starved, Claire added, 'But no one cooks like you, Blodwen. It's so good to be home.' There was only the slightest hesitation on the last word, and she felt Martin's hand squeeze her shoulder in support.

Blodwen put a finger to her lips.

'Your grandmother is in the garden trying to pretend she hasn't been looking at her watch every five minutes since we had our lunch. Martin can come into the kitchen with me while I put the kettle on, and you go through and let her know you've arrived.'

Claire tossed her cap onto the hall table and, crossing the morning room, paused at the french windows for a moment to watch her grandmother pruning the winter jasmine. It was oddly reassuring to see her occupied with such a mundane task. Civilization might be at stake, but the jasmine still needed to be pruned. There might be vegetables at its roots instead of flower beds, but some things did not change.

As though sensing that she was being watched, Mrs Grant turned, glancing towards the house.

'Claire! Well . . . you've arrived at last, then.' The words were said crisply and without apparent emotion. However, with a heightened awareness, Claire was able to recognize the restraint as an ingrained part of her grandmother's character, just as she could discern the affection in the faded blue eyes.

'Wonderful to be home again,' she said, and this time she really meant it. 'But isn't it getting a bit cold for you to be out in the garden?'

'I'm not in my dotage yet, you know.' The words were spoken without a smile.

It occurred to Claire that not so long ago such a remark might have crushed rather than amused her. She chuckled, and kissed her grandmother warmly. They went inside, their arms linked.

Blodwen had brewed the tea, and Martin was making toast through the glowing bars of the range. Claire sat beside him on the rug, warming her hands at the fire. Shortage of fuel had made the old-fashioned kitchen the most used room in the house.

It had been a warm day for early spring but now that the sun was low on the horizon, the clear sky held the chill promise of frost. The warmth of the fire made Claire yawn.

'Are you trying to tell me something?' Martin said, grinning. 'I can take a hint, you know.'

'Chump!' she said. 'I came off night watch at eight this morning. I feel a bit jaded. A bath will perk me up.'

'You'll stay to dinner, Martin?' Mrs Grant said.

'Thank you, I wish I could, but the Baldwins are expecting me to dine there tonight.' He finished toasting the last piece of bread and got to his feet. 'I'll have that cup of tea and then I must make a move.' Turning to Claire, he added, 'And you look as though you could use a good night's sleep.'

Claire tried not to look disappointed. She had hoped they might spend the evening together, but she accepted that he could hardly alter all his arrangements just because he had discovered that she would be home.

When, a little later, she went to the door to see him out, he kissed the tip of her nose. 'I'll call you tomorrow,' he said. 'Hope to see you before I go. We must manage things better next time.'

The old easy relationship was back in gear. She watched as he crossed the road and turned the corner at the top of the hill. For the first time in over two years Claire was happy to be alive.

2

Claire was in her bedroom when Blodwen put her head around the door on the pretext of being on her way to check that there was sufficient hot water.

'Hasn't he grown into a handsome young man, then?' she said, smoothing the bath sheet draped over her arm.

'I've seen worse,' Claire admitted. 'I wonder if his father is also going to dine with the Baldwins tonight.'

'You didn't know?' Blodwen was wide-eyed with surprise. 'His father is back in the Army.'

'But I thought he came out for good before the war, the year Martin's mother became ill. Isn't he rather old to be joining up again?'

'Not too old . . . not now. At the War Office he is.'

'You mean Martin's on his own in that barn of a house?' Claire looked aghast.

'No, fach. The house was commandeered for the military. He usually goes to London to stay with his father, but Roy Baldwin's parents asked him to stay with them this weekend.'

'So, *they* managed to keep in touch,' Claire said, slightly peeved.

'Well, that wasn't very difficult. Roy and Martin joined up at the same time and after their training they were sent to the same squadron. Roy couldn't get away this time.' Blodwen retreated to the bathroom across the landing, calling: 'I'm running your bath. Come along now before it gets cold.'

After a bath and a light meal Claire was ready for bed, but she was awake early on Saturday morning and after breakfast found herself waiting for the telephone to ring. This fact did not escape her grandmother who kept her busy with small tasks around the house, but when midday approached without any contact she called Claire in from the garden where she was hanging out some washing.

'If you've nothing better to do, I wish you'd take this letter to the post for me.'

Claire glanced at the clock. Martin had said he'd be in touch, but she wasn't going to bank on it. In the past he had whistled and expected her to come running. If that was what he expected now, he'd have to think again.

'Of course,' she said, taking the envelope from the outstretched hand. 'I may be a while. I could do with a breath of sea air.'

The sun was shining fitfully from a cloudy sky as she climbed over the brow of the hill and took the turning down towards the cluster of shops she knew so well: the old-fashioned pharmacy which smelt of a mixture of cloves and cinnamon, with a hint of pine disinfectant intermingled with the gentle scent of soap; the grocer's shop with tall round-seated chairs set against a polished counter, with its opposite counter scrubbed white but now minus the array of cheeses and succulent cooked meats; the sweet shop whose striped mint humbugs and treacle toffee had so often taken all her pocket money, and whose ice-cream had been a local legend. She paused outside the half-boarded window. The empty jars were an added reminder that there was a war on.

Dropping her grandmother's letter into the post-box she walked on, unthinking, not registering the route she was taking, the familiar route to her old home.

Her mind free-wheeled. A good night's sleep had left her completely relaxed. She stopped, suddenly realizing that her hand was reaching out for a gate no longer there.

The shock made her cry out.

She was back in the splintered darkness of that terrible night, trapped under the protecting door and the sliding rubble where the blast had flung her, calling out for the reassuring sounds of life . . . which never came. As though they were before her eyes, she saw the torn bodies, no longer human, twisted into impossible attitudes, yet seeming to move in the flickering light of burning debris.

The nightmare had become reality.

'Claire!' It was Martin's voice close behind her. 'You shouldn't have come here on your own.'

'I didn't plan to come this way.'

'Why didn't you wait for me?'

'It was getting late. I thought you'd changed your mind.'

'Sorry, Claire. My fault. The Baldwins wanted to chat and it was difficult to get away.'

He wasn't looking in her direction. It was clear that he too was finding it disturbing to perceive the extent of the destruction, and to see his own home next door still with some of the windows boarded up, and Army trucks parked where the flower beds once flourished.

'I was day dreaming, I suppose,' Claire said. 'Just not thinking where I was going. It was such a shock coming up against it like that.'

'Is this the first time you've seen it since the bombing?'

'Yes.' She had turned away, but she glanced back over her shoulder. 'Without actually seeing it, I could almost fool myself that it hadn't happened. I didn't have to accept the reality.'

'And have you accepted it now, Claire?'

There was a long pause before she replied. 'I'm . . . perhaps . . . half way there.'

'It'll never hit you like that a second time.'

'No. I don't believe it will.'

'I don't make a habit of coming this way myself,' he confessed. 'I rang to speak to you, and your grandmother said you'd gone for a walk. I decided to take a short cut to the shore. I thought I might find you there.'

'You didn't expect to find me here?'

'I'm glad I did. Time to move on. You've had enough for one day.'

They walked to the end of the road, turning down the steep slope to the promenade and across the sand, out to the water's edge. In the distance, as far as Claire could see, the sand looked firm and smooth, the blemishes eliminated by the receding tide.

'If only life could be like that,' she said, staring at the flat stretch of shore, mesmerised by the regular ebb and flow of the tide.

'A fresh start every time; everything wiped away.'

Martin frowned. 'A blank? Never to remember the good times? That wouldn't suit me . . . or you, Claire.'

'If only I *could* remember the good times.'

'You will.'

His confidence made her turn to scan the houses overlooking the mouth of the river, but there was no magic transformation, the happy past seemed beyond recall.

She was suddenly very much aware that Martin was standing close beside her, looking down at her with a concentration which she found disturbing.

'Odd,' he said thoughtfully. 'I know more about the Mess cooks than I know about you.'

'Well! Lucky you!'

'Don't be coy, Claire. It doesn't suit you.'

She was on firmer ground now. That was more like the old Martin. One year her senior, he had always been like a bossy elder brother. Her response, as in the past, was swift.

'You've done nothing but criticize since you met me at the station. I'm not fifteen now, you know.'

'And don't sulk,' he said. 'That's one stage worse.'

'Don't leave home; don't grieve; don't sulk! Can I do anything right?' She was hurt and angry, but she could see from the grin on Martin's face that he was congratulating himself on jolting her back to the present. For that she knew she had cause to thank him.

'I'm serious, Claire. If you can't get out of the Service you should put in for a compassionate posting nearer home.' He glanced at his watch. 'And I must move. I didn't realize it was getting so late. Mrs Baldwin is making an early lunch. I've got a train to catch.'

They hurried back up the hill.

'I wish we had more time,' he said.

'And I suppose you'd go on nagging me about that posting?'

'Yes.'

'Then perhaps it's just as well you're going back this afternoon.'

'You really are a chip off the old block,' he said, grinning.

They had reached the Baldwins' house.

'Goodbye, Martin,' Claire said, waving to Mrs Baldwin who was beckoning him to hurry.

'Put in for that posting,' he said, planting a swift kiss on her cheek as she turned away.

'Don't you ever give up?'

'Not without a struggle. If you finish lunch in time, come and see me off.'

She pretended not to hear.

* * *

'And what's the matter with you, my girl?' Blodwen said, clearing the dining table after Claire had shown little appetite for lunch. 'Of course! He's going back to his squadron this afternoon. Never you mind. You'll see each other again soon.'

Claire followed her into the kitchen.

'Not if I can help it. He still thinks he can try to run my life.'

'That shows he cares what happens to you.'

'It's not me he's worried about.'

'No? Well, you know best, I suppose.' Blodwen looked up at the kitchen clock. 'One fifty-five I think the train was. He called it thirteen fifty-five, but apparently it means the same thing. Just about have time to get there.' Her tone was off-hand, simply giving a throwaway piece of information.

Claire picked up a dish-cloth, and put it down again. Martin would be flying — perhaps tomorrow. She might never see him again.

'Oh, get on with you,' Blodwen said

impatiently, pushing her away from the sink. 'You know you want to see him off. Mind, you'll have to hurry. His train goes from Lime Street. He's getting a lift from one of his pals somewhere down the line.'

★ ★ ★

The ferry would take too long. Claire ran all the way to the terminus of the Mersey Railway to catch the train which took her, stop by interminable stop, through the tunnel beneath the river.

Coming up the steps from the underground station to the busy street, she ran into the middle of the road and swung on to a passing tram to gain a few precious minutes.

Lime Street Station was crowded, and time was ticking by as she found the right platform.

'Can I go through?' she asked the ticket collector.

'You're too late, love.'

She stood behind the barrier, watching as the train curved out of sight.

'That's the trouble with these days,' the man said gruffly, but with sympathy in his eyes. 'Too many bloody Goodbyes.'

★ ★ ★

Mrs Grant, sitting in her favourite armchair, put her newspaper down and peered over the top of her spectacles.

'You got there in time, I take it?'

Claire shook her head.

'A pity to allow a slight difference of opinion to spoil a friendship.'

'Just because he's your blue-eyed boy . . . '

'Dark brown, I believe.'

'You know perfectly well what I mean. He's infuriating.'

'I thought him quite charming. I must say he's turned out better than I ever imagined. He was an odious child.'

'I'd like to tell him that,' Claire said with a smile.

'Tell him, by all means. I fancy you'd be wasting your time. I made no secret of my feelings.'

'True. He used to be scared of you. That was quite an achievement; you were the only person who ever managed it.'

Mrs Grant straightened, her face a blank of disbelief.

It was Claire's turn to be surprised. 'Don't tell me you didn't know! We were all terrified of you. You could be quite fierce at times.'

'Was I *too* strict?' Her grandmother seemed to shrink in her chair.

'No,' Claire said, regretting her candour. 'And terrified is the wrong word. But you did make us toe the line.' She touched her grandmother's cheek, remembering with sadness how alien they had been in the past. 'We were a wild bunch.'

'I couldn't bear to think I had cast a shadow over Peter's young life.'

'Darling! Peter adored you. You know he did.'

It was true. Peter and his grandmother had had a very special relationship. Whereas Claire had flinched under the barbed tongue, her brother had bounced back, always ready for more.

In the days that followed, Claire was increasingly aware that her grandmother had lost some of her normal resilience. It made her wonder if Martin might, after all, have been right.

When questioned, Blodwen at first refused to be drawn, but finally she admitted that she was worried.

'She'll be mad with me for discussing it with you. I think it's her heart. But, will she see a doctor?' She shook her head. 'I've begged her, and bullied her. I wish you'd have a word.'

But Claire had no more success than Blodwen. It was only on the morning of her departure that a crack appeared in the proud facade.

'I shall miss you so much, Claire,' her grandmother said. 'I feel we are really getting to know one another at last.'

Blodwen mopped her eyes. 'Goodbye, Claire fach,' she said. 'And do remember to air your things now, won't you?'

'I'll try. Goodbye, Blodwen.'

She turned again to her grandmother. For a brief moment they clung to each other, and then Claire continued down the path and out of the gate.

'Look after her, Blodwen,' she called, looking back over her shoulder, waving until she was beyond their sight.

3

The watery sun had gone down by the time Claire boarded the train on the single-track railway. Long delays had caused her to miss the scheduled connections, and she was tired and hungry when, at last, she stepped down onto the platform at Danborough.

'Is there anyone else for the camp?' she asked the ticket collector.

'Nay, lass,' he said. 'Reckon you'd better go to the canteen over t'road. Like as not, there'll be someone there who'll give you a lift. Not a night for a walk.' He looked up at the darkening sky.

A heavy drizzle veiled the moors.

The canteen was empty. As Claire closed the door a woman came from behind a curtain at the other side of the counter.

'I didn't expect to see anyone tonight,' she said, smiling. 'You've come off the train, have you?'

Claire nodded. 'Just my luck. I'm the only one.'

'It's been tippling down since tea-time. What can I get you?'

'I'm starving,' Claire said. 'I should have

had plenty of time for a meal on the way, but the trains were late all along the line.'

'Poached egg on toast do you?'

Claire's eyes lit up. Had the woman suggested scrambled egg it could well have been a rubbery concoction of powdered egg, but poached egg had to be the genuine article. Quite a rarity.

The woman was not slow to appreciate Claire's reaction. 'I've always kept a few hens in the back garden,' she said, putting a large slice of home-made bread under the grill, and taking two eggs from a bowl at the end of the counter. 'They lay well. Now that I'm on my own I don't need all the eggs. My lad's in the Navy, and Arthur — that's my husband,' she explained with a faraway look in her eyes, 'he was at Tunis. God knows where he is now.'

'You must be proud of him,' Claire said.

'Aye,' the woman conceded, almost reluctantly. 'I'm proud of them both. But my Arthur didn't *have* to go, not at his age, and I think all the more of him for that.' She glanced up at the clock on the wall. 'I'll send someone along to the pub to see if there's a truck down from the camp.'

Claire had polished off the poached eggs, followed by a piece of treacle tart — the great standby of most canteens — and was finishing her second cup of coffee when the door of the canteen opened and an RAF corporal came in, big leather gauntlets tucked under one arm.

'Did you think you were going to have to walk it?' he asked with a chuckle.

'It did cross my mind.'

'Must be your lucky day.' He tossed his cap and gauntlets onto one of the tables. 'The fuel feed's been playing up, otherwise I'd have been back at camp hours ago. I'll just get a cuppa and a wad, then we'll get cracking. Not fit for a dog this weather.'

Like two different worlds, Claire thought as the truck rocked and bumped up the steep hill; like moving from one existence into another.

The rain was heavier now, beating on the windscreen. It was cold, more like winter than spring. They stopped at the Guard Room to check in. It was impossible to see the low wooden buildings in the dim light of the masked headlamps.

'I'll drop you off at the Waafery,' the corporal said. 'I've got to go past there anyway.'

Claire was glad to get inside the hut, although the blue-tinted electric light bulb swinging in the draught made a depressing welcome. She walked down the narrow passage to the room she shared with three other members of 'C' Crew.

'Claire!' Edna, who looked after them all in a bossy but kindly way, got up from the floor where she had been using the heat from the black iron stove to dry her hair. 'We made up your bed. Pat remembered that you'd be back tonight. Trust you to miss domestic evening.'

'I thought the smell of polish was a bit strong.'

'How's your granny?' Barbara asked, spearing her knitting needles into the ball of wool on her bed.

Claire had to smile at the thought of her grandmother's expression if she could have heard herself referred to in that way.

'What's so funny?' Barbara said.

'You'd have to know my grandmother to appreciate that. She's not exactly the 'granny' type.'

'Well, how is she anyway?'

Claire frowned. 'Truth is, I'm worried about her. I think I may have to apply for a posting nearer home.'

'Must you?' Edna said. 'We're so short of good operators. We're on a three-watch system now. Brace yourself. We have the usual one-to-six watch on the first day — thirteen to eighteen hundred hours.'

'Breaks you in gently,' Barbara said, without enthusiasm. 'That's what we're on tomorrow.'

'Then eight-to-one: o-eight hundred the next morning until thirteen hundred,' Edna continued. 'Afternoon off, when I have to make sure you miserable lot get a bit of exercise and some rest — no sloping off for a crafty afternoon out; then on again at eighteen hundred that evening, until o-eight hundred the following morning.'

'Fourteen hours!' Pat emphasized, propping herself up in bed. 'It nearly kills me.'

She looked about twelve, tucked between the sheets with her baby-blonde hair done up in curlers.

'You wouldn't believe she's been in bed for most of today, would you?' Barbara said.

'Well, you know what I'm like. I *need* my sleep.'

'You can say that again,' Edna said, laughing. 'The dormouse of 'C' Crew.'

Pat pulled a face and slid beneath the blankets.

Barbara poked the dying embers of the fire into life and lifted the lid of the kettle which was sitting on top of the stove with a feeble wisp of steam coming out of the spout.

'Shall I brew up?' she said. 'This is the last of today's fuel ration. You'll have to get into

33

bed if you want to keep warm. With luck, there's just about enough life left to boil the kettle.'

Waiting for the tea to brew, Claire began unpacking. Even Pat revived at the sight of one of Blodwen's fruit cakes. Claire had been reluctant to accept it because she knew that precious points from the ration books would have been surrendered for the fruit, and that other ingredients would have come from the frugal weekly allocation. However, Blodwen took great pride in her management of the meagre rations, and a rejection would have caused great offence. As some form of compensation, Claire was already planning a letter telling Blodwen of 'C' Crew's appreciation.

* * *

Coming off the one-to-six watch the following evening, Claire felt as though she had never been away. The real world seemed now to be within the confines of the barbed-wire fence.

Twenty-four hours later, having already worked the eight-to-one morning watch, 'C' Crew were on duty again. The first part of the night watch proved busy — so much easier to cope with than long stretches of inactivity.

Despite the fact that the constant search for enemy aircraft was always maintained, there was the possibility that concentration might lapse during a lull. To a great extent this danger was avoided by the hourly changeover when each member of the crew performed a different role. An hour was quite long enough to be watching the trace of light flickering across the cathode ray tube.

Gradually activity diminished. The sergeant looked at the clock. 'Right,' he said. 'Start changing over. Barbara, you take over the tube. Claire can plot. Pat . . . teller, and Edna, you record.'

George, the only male operator on the watch, spoke into his head-set: 'Hello, Midcastle. Changing over.' He unplugged the lead, and Barbara slipped into the chair as he got up.

The uneven trace across the cathode ray tube showed only the normal reflections from sea and land, no enemy activity. With her left hand turning the knob of the goniometer Barbara searched the sky, sweeping through their segment of the North Sea, altering the arrangement of the aerials to check and counter-check.

'I'll make a cuppa,' George said. It was his hour off. The brew he produced was a scalding concoction of cocoa and condensed milk. 'Guaranteed to take the skin off your nose and make your hands like velvet,' he said, passing round the mugs.

His timing was perfect. Not many minutes later Barbara called out: 'I think I've got something — almost off the end of the tube. It's very faint.' She paused. 'And it's showing IFF.'

IFF — identification friend or foe — the small flashing blip of light showed that the aircraft was friendly. Almost at the limit of their equipment, it was a weak signal.

Barbara marked the range and, turning the goniometer, got as accurate a bearing as she could. The screen above her head transcribed the information.

'Danborough. New plot. Charlie niner-fife-seven-zero. One aircraft showing IFF.' Pat, no dormouse now, passed on the information to Group Headquarters where it would be transferred to a large plotting table showing all the air activity around the coast and overland. With a chinagraph pencil Claire marked the plot on the perspex-covered map, and Edna put it down on the record sheet.

The line to the Group plotting room was suddenly very much alive, with plots and identifications being exchanged without pause.

'It'll be the first of those bombers that

went out earlier,' one of the mechanics said. 'They'll be coming back about now.'

Soon the tube showed numerous aircraft, some in groups, some singly.

'Danborough. New Plot. Charlie six-zero-seven-fife. Two aircraft. No IFF. Height 18,000 feet.'

'Check the height of that last plot, Danborough.'

Already concentrating on another formation, Barbara quickly double-checked.

'Hello Midcastle,' she said. 'That last plot — 18,000 feet.'

'Hostile two seven, Danborough,' the Group plotter replied, giving the identification.

The plotting was complicated: a tangle of friendly and hostile aircraft coming towards the coast, with the fighters coming from further south to intercept the enemy. In such conditions it needed skill to separate the aircraft, to make sense of the abundance of information.

At the next changeover Claire was on the tube. The steady drone of the plots continued until, suddenly, she interrupted: 'Broad IFF at fifty miles. I think I can get a fix.'

A Mayday signal. The identification signal in the aircraft could be switched over to give an SOS. Instead of a small flick of light every two-and-a-half seconds, the flashing signal expanded to take up ten miles of the calibrated trace. With luck, it gave the radar operator the opportunity to pin-point the aircraft's position so that, should it ditch, Air Sea Rescue could be directed to the right spot. Minutes could be vital in a cold, hostile sea.

'That's as near as I can get it,' Claire said as the teller passed on the information. 'It's faded. Nothing there now.'

The atmosphere was tense.

The sergeant bent over her shoulder. 'You're sure it was broad IFF — a genuine Mayday?'

'Yes, I'm sure.'

'It could be a fault on the aircraft transmitter.'

'It didn't look like faulty IFF,' Claire said, vainly searching for another signal. She was thinking that it could be Martin out there, ditching in the North Sea.

'Telephone for you, Sarge,' one of the mechanics called urgently.

Returning moments later to check the screen, the sergeant said: 'Concentrate on the broad IFF.'

Claire willed the broad blip to reappear — even a hint of the distress signal — but there was nothing.

38

The changeover came again on the hour. Claire felt drained, but she would have preferred to have had something to do. The customary hour off after the eye-straining session on the tube gave her too much time to think. A fighter, or a bomber? A rubber dinghy on the sea? There could be one man, or several, fighting for survival. Now it seemed altogether more personal. Now it could be Martin.

She collected the mugs and did the washing-up; anything to keep occupied.

The activity around the coast was clearing and soon all was quiet once more. The operator on the tube kept up a constant watch. Knitting needles clicked — Barbara's method of keeping herself awake after twelve hours on duty. The blank recording sheet was on the table at her elbow.

The German reconnaissance aircraft, Weather Willie, made the customary early morning check of the conditions over the North Sea, this time without tangling with any opposition from the RAF. It was an operation as regular as clockwork.

At last the relief crew took over. It was time to climb into the truck and go down to the living site for breakfast. As 'C' Crew were about to leave, the CO, arrived.

'Sergeant,' he said, nodding his head in the

direction of his office next to the operations room.

'Sir.'

'What does the old man want at this time of the morning?' George mumbled under his breath as the door closed. 'I'm ready for a bit of kip.'

'Aren't we all?' Pat yawned.

The door opened again.

'Grant,' the CO said. 'You'll be glad to know that Air Sea Rescue picked up a crew from the sea this morning, almost spot-on that plot of yours. Well done.'

'Thank you, sir.'

It was a jubilant crew that went down to the cookhouse for breakfast. The weariness of fourteen hours in the tense atmosphere of the operations block vanished. Claire slept well that morning. It was rare to get such a positive result from a night's work. Somehow it seemed to redress the balance, if only fractionally. She was beginning to surface when Edna, usually the first up, came in with the mail.

'Letter for you, Claire,' she said, dropping an envelope on her pillow.

Raising herself on one elbow, Claire frowned, trying to recognize the writing. It was not from her grandmother or Blodwen, and the postmark was smudged. Puzzled, she slid a nailfile under the flap.

'Martin wants to meet me in York,' she said. 'He's going to ring me here.'

'You'll get a rocket if he does,' Edna said. 'You know what they're like about personal calls.'

He did ring. Claire didn't get the call, but she did get the rocket.

Martin wrote again, this time asking her to ring the Mess. This meant a long walk to the village telephone kiosk. Trunk calls were subject to long delays. Twice she waited for over an hour only to find that Martin was not available. At the end of the week on her third attempt he was at the other end of the line.

'Claire! At last! I thought I was getting the brush-off.'

'You should try getting through.'

'I did. Remember?'

'From the comfort of the Mess, no doubt. I was thinking of bringing my bed down to the village telephone kiosk.'

'Any chance of getting a forty-eight for next weekend,' he said. 'I could meet you in York?'

'Not a hope.'

'Why?'

'You should know better than to ask.'

'You're not against the idea in principle?'

'No,' she said, smiling to herself, wondering when he was going to get round to the question of her posting.

There was a crossed line and they could barely hear each other. Precious moments were wasted.

'Can you hear me now?' Martin said.

'That's better.'

'If you can't make York, how about us applying for leave at the same time?'

'I've only just come back from leave,' Claire said.

'I'm talking about the summer.'

The line crackled and a voice said, 'Your time is up, caller,' and without the option of paying for another three minutes they were cut off.

Angry and frustrated, Claire walked back up the hill. After calling into the Orderly Room to check when she was next due for some leave, she started a letter to Martin giving provisional dates. It was not an easy letter to write. She suspected his motives. It was almost certainly a ploy to get her back with her grandmother.

She tore up one letter after another. The one she finally put in the mail box was stilted, like a letter to a stranger.

★ ★ ★

As the weeks went by and the time of her leave approached, Claire had confirmation that Martin would be there too, and she wondered if it was all a big mistake. There was little time to brood on this. The camp had its own routine, reinforced by isolation, and everyone was feeling the pressure of long hours and complete concentration.

'We're in the buried reserve tonight,' Edna said as they were preparing to go on watch one evening.

'Oh, no!' Claire groaned. She could remember the thrill of excitement she had felt when she first encountered the underground site, the entrance almost hidden in the heather. However, it was no Aladdin's cave, and the novelty had very quickly worn off. 'That place is like a mausoleum.'

'I couldn't agree more.' Edna led the way out of the Waafery and onto the moorland track which led to the technical site. 'Am I right in thinking you've seen the Queen Bee about the posting?'

'Yes. She wants me to wait until I've been home again and seen how things are. I suppose a posting will be easier now that the new operators have come from the Radio School.'

'They're a bit green, but at least we're back on a four watch system.'

They joined the remainder of the crew and George led the way through the heather, past the tall aerials, stopping beside a large slab of stone which looked as though it had been there forever.

'Bloody buried reserve,' he mumbled, picking up an iron bar half hidden in the undergrowth and striking the stone twice. 'Take a good deep breath of fresh air. That's all you'll get until twenty-three hundred hours.'

There was a pause, and then a voice called from the depths, 'Five.'

'Oh . . . Hell's teeth!' George shoved his forage cap to the back of his head. 'Anyone remember the number?'

Barbara pushed him aside. 'Nine,' she called, bending over the stone, the sum of the numbers making the pass number for the day.

The stone rolled to one side, with a little help from George.

'Phew! Take a niff of that! A subtle blend of polish, sweat and chemical closet,' he said, standing back and letting the girls go down the iron ladder first.

After the freshness of the moors it was difficult to ignore the heavy atmosphere. At the bottom of the narrow shaft it took a few minutes for their eyes to get accustomed to the semi-darkness of the operations room, a bleak square floored with shiny brown linoleum and dominated by the massive receiver.

The changeover completed, they settled into the routine of searching for enemy activity. For a while there was none.

George broke the monotony by passing round the latest snaps of his children. He was very much a family man.

'The wife tells me Bobby's just starting to talk,' he said and, looking away, blew his nose, loud and long. 'I miss them, and that's the truth.'

'You're from Kent, aren't you, George?' Claire said, trying to picture him as a father who loved his children, not simply as a rather scruffy airman.

He nodded. 'They're down in Devon now with the wife's parents. It's safer there.'

And then the first tiny blip appeared at the extreme range of the trace, and then another, and another. The Luftwaffe had taken to the air.

'Hostile three-seven.' The identification came over the line. 'Estimated number please, Danborough.'

Barbara studied the weak signals. 'Two . . . no, three. And three more. It's getting difficult to separate them,' she said, narrowing her eyes. 'As near as I can say, ten plus.'

One aircraft produced a steady blip; two gave an even beat; a formation needed the eye of an experienced operator.

Gradually, the formation came towards the coast, the first of many. It was going to be a busy night. The fighters had already closed with the enemy, the IFF signals singling them out from the German bombers.

'They usually turn north before that,' Claire said, plotting the next formation approaching the coast.

The sergeant studied the map and went to ring the CO. The relief crew had arrived and were getting a general view of things before taking over.

The telephone rang.

'Red alert!' the sergeant called, putting down the receiver. 'Steel helmets on. Get that changeover completed. Come on 'C' Crew, fast as you can. No lights on the transport. Get cracking.'

It was a bomber's moon. The truck driver had no great difficulty in following the road to the living site. A dull throbbing drone came closer and louder every moment, and then all hell let loose. The scream of dive-bombers rent the air.

Strategically placed sandbags gave limited cover on the living site. Wooden buildings offered no protection. The huge aerials stood out like welcoming signposts in the moonlight but, if the Germans were running true to form, they would target the living site as well as the operational buildings. Outside the cookhouse Claire stood with the rest of the crew, waiting for the attack to begin. The strap of her steel helmet cut into her chin. It was the moment she had been dreading. The moment of truth. But there was no panic. Fear gripped her by the throat but, beneath it all, she was calm.

'Get down!' someone shouted as the bombers once more howled from the sky to skim the rooftops.

As one person, they threw themselves to the ground. The noise was deafening and continuous. The thin whistles of the bombs followed in quick succession as, one after another, the bombers swooped to kill.

The light anti-aircraft cover was no match for the skilled pilots whose speed at low level made the gunners' task almost impossible.

Then, quite suddenly, it was over. Anti-climax. The tearing fury of the laboured engines gave way to a steady beating note, becoming fainter with every second.

One by one, feeling rather foolish, they got to their feet.

'I'm glad I didn't press that lot yesterday,'

George said, rubbing the dirt off his battledress. 'Rum do, that. Half the bloody bombs didn't explode.'

'D'you think they want us off the air, but not off the map?' Edna said.

'Could be. Maybe they're going to drop in on us later.'

Was that why the RAF Regiment had been teaching them how to fire a rifle? Claire wondered.

'Well, I'm having my supper first,' Pat said, yawning. 'And then I'm going to bed.'

There had been no casualties, but the moors surrounding the camp were littered with unexploded bombs and by the middle of the next day the bomb disposal squad had arrived. They were still there the following week when Claire picked up her pass and travel warrant from the Orderly Room. There had been no more attacks but security was tighter than ever, and Claire had half expected her leave to be cancelled.

'There's your ration card,' the clerk said. 'And I'm just dishing out the soap coupons, so you'd better take yours now.'

'Thanks,' Claire said, hurrying to catch the ration wagon which would drop her at the station.

'Have a good leave,' Edna called as they

passed at the door. 'And . . . Claire . . . '

'Yes?'

'Have fun.'

Claire laughed. 'I might surprise you and do just that,' she said, crossing to the Guard Room to book out.

4

This time, Claire's arrival at Lime Street Station held something of the old excitement: the shadows, if not completely banished, were very much in the background.

The train pulled in at the open platform where the taxis queued.

Martin had already seen her, and he hurried to open the door.

'I've got a taxi waiting,' he said, taking the holdall from her hand and dropping it at his feet, intent on giving her a quick hug and a brotherly peck on the cheek. 'Any luck with the posting?'

'Not, 'Welcome home, Claire. Good to see you',' she said with a wry smile as they walked across the platform to board the waiting taxi, which immediately pulled out ahead of the queue. 'Anyway, how did you know I'd applied for a posting? Did Blodwen tell you?'

'No. But I guessed she might have written.'

'Did you put her up to it? Martin, you really are the limit!'

'Not guilty,' he said. 'But you haven't seen them lately, have you?'

50

'You know I haven't.' She looked at him uncertainly. 'Blodwen told me that she was worried about Grandmother, but there didn't seem to be any urgency. Is she worse?'

'You'll have to judge for yourself.'

She couldn't make out whether he was simply pressing home his original biased view, or if he had good reason for this continued campaign. For the last part of the journey their conversation stuck on small talk.

When the taxi slowed as they approached the house Claire tried hard not to show her dismay at the sight of her grandmother and Blodwen standing at the gate. Her grandmother, leaning heavily on a stick, looked frail, her complexion almost transparent. The customary elegance and poise were absent. Blodwen too had changed, and this was almost more of a shock. Instead of the usual rosy complexion, her skin had a grey pallor, and there was about her an air of fatigue which Claire had never seen before.

'We've had the flu,' Blodwen explained later when they were having tea.

'Well, you're going to have a rest while I'm here,' Claire insisted.

'So, you think I can't manage. Is that it?' Blodwen said indignantly.

Martin cut in, hoping to avert a conflict:

'You remember the cottage which Father bought in North Wales, hoping that Mother could convalesce there?'

'Yes, of course,' Mrs Grant said. 'A bit of a white elephant, I imagine.'

'It was hardly used until Father had it sorted out a few months ago.'

'And promptly let it to a family from Liverpool,' Mrs Grant added acidly. 'I thought the idea was to give you a home.'

'Yes, that was the idea, but we both agreed that it seemed wrong to allow it to stand empty for the greater part of the year, especially when these people needed a break. They'd had a tough time in the blitz and the woman was heading for a breakdown. Anyway, it must have done the trick. They went back to Liverpool a few weeks ago. They were missing their friends — not to mention the local fish and chip shop.'

'So, the house is empty again?' Claire said.

'Father's been staying there himself for the last couple of weeks.'

'He's on leave?'

'He went back to London this morning.'

'I seem to remember that your mother's family originally came from Wales. Isn't that so?' Mrs Grant said.

He nodded. 'If she'd recovered, I think they'd have settled there for good.'

'So, where are you staying?' Claire asked.

'I'm with the Baldwins overnight, but Father suggested that I should spend my leave at the cottage. Keep the place aired.'

So much for synchronizing their leave. Claire felt sick with disappointment.

'But, of course,' she said, forcing herself to smile. 'It's your home, after all.'

'It has four bedrooms — not very big, but completely furnished: linen, everything.' He looked first at Mrs Grant and then at Blodwen. 'Come with me?'

'You don't want old bodies like us around,' Blodwen said.

'I think Martin knows what he's about,' Mrs Grant said, giving him a very straight look.

'I know you wouldn't allow Claire to come on her own, if that's what you mean.'

'Exactly. That would be out of the question.'

'Then, say you'll come.'

The gap in the conversation gave Claire the chance to ask, 'Am I to be consulted?'

'Claire!' Martin looked shattered. 'I thought . . .'

'Whistle and she'll come running. That's what you thought. Don't deny it. Just like

53

the old days. Well, I'm not fifteen any more, and I do have a mind of my own.'

'Oh, yes indeed! A chip off the old block,' he said under his breath, glancing at Mrs Grant, whose controlled expression told him that she had heard, and was perhaps more amused than affronted.

'A change of air would be very pleasant,' she said vaguely.

It was just that vagueness which caught Claire's attention. So uncharacteristic. She would have welcomed the more familiar brusqueness. It was clear that a holiday in the country was exactly what her grandmother and Blodwen needed.

'Then, what are we waiting for?' she said, and smiled as she heard Martin's low whistle of relief.

'What do we do about food?' asked Blodwen, practical as ever. 'We've already got our rations for this week.'

'Quite simple. We can take those with us.' Mrs Grant pursed her lips. 'A small paper bag would take the lot.'

'Our ration cards can be used at the village shop,' Martin said, glancing at Claire.

'We'll travel light,' Mrs Grant said. 'I understand that public transport can be somewhat unreliable these days.'

'Don't worry. I'll take care of everything,'

Martin said. 'Can you be ready about eleven tomorrow morning?'

★ ★ ★

The following morning, Martin took one look at the line of suitcases in the hall. 'This is what you call travelling light?' he said, piling them into the waiting taxi.

Mrs Grant pulled on her gloves. 'Nothing superfluous, I assure you,' she said, smoothing each finger.

'Bucket and spade?' he asked, his face serious, as he lifted the last two bags.

'There now!' She clucked her tongue. 'I was so sure you'd have brought your own.'

'Will you two stop fooling about,' Claire said, only too happy to see them sparring again. 'We'll miss our train.'

Breaking the journey at Chester for a light meal, they took an early afternoon connection, a slow train following the coastline of North Wales.

'I do hope they'll be all right,' Claire whispered to Martin, watching her grandmother and Blodwen dozing in the seats opposite.

'We're almost there. The change of scene will do the trick.'

An express buffeted past the windows

waking the two sleepers.

'Well, I never!' Blodwen rubbed her eyes. 'Trains always send me to sleep. Miss the station I would if I was on my own.'

The train passed underneath a footbridge and pulled up a short distance down the line.

'This is it,' Martin said, getting down the luggage from the rack and opening the carriage door.

The solitary figure chatting to the engine driver at the far end of the platform saw the train on its way. On his return to the ticket barrier he picked up two of the larger suitcases. His duties appeared to include everything from Station Master to porter.

'Is there a taxi about?' Martin asked.

'Evans the taxi?' The man laughed. 'You'd have to go a mighty long way to find him. No taxi now. Driving a tank in the desert he is. Now, where was it you were wanting to go?'

'The White Cottage.'

'The Colonel's house? Ty Gwyn?'

'You know it?'

'Yes indeed.' The man's voice was guarded. 'You going to see him then?'

'No. My father won't be there now, but we shall be staying for a few days.'

'Your father! Of course. I can see the

56

resemblance now.' Natural caution allayed, his manner changed from polite suspicion to friendly helpfulness. 'You carry on. I'll get the boy to bring the bags up directly.' He pointed along the lane. 'You can see the roof from here. If you cut through by the chapel it only takes a couple of minutes.'

The walk to the White Cottage took them past the plain brickbuilt chapel with its slate roof, through the kissing gate to the footpath worn bare across the meadow of lush grass. The limewashed cottage stood out, bright in the sun.

Mrs Grant and Blodwen walked up the path while Claire and Martin lingered at the gate.

'It was a wonderful idea, Martin,' Claire said, her enthusiasm smothering any remaining doubts.

'Glad you approve.' Half playfully, his lips brushed her brow.

A low whistle made them turn around.

'Your sweetheart, is it?' asked the urchin in patched knee-length shorts, his woollen socks concertinaed around his ankles.

'You mind your own business,' Martin said, grinning broadly. Then, seeing the trolley with their luggage, he fished in his pocket for some loose change. 'That was quick work,' he said, slipping some coins

57

into the boy's hand. 'What's your name?'

The boy looked down at his hand and whistled again. 'Thanks,' he said, his face splitting wide with a smile. 'I'm Ivor.'

He heaved one of the cases from the trolley and marched up the path to the front door where Mrs Grant and Blodwen were standing. Lifting the latch, he pushed the door open with his foot and waited for them to go inside.

'Not locked?' Mrs Grant said, frowning at such an oversight.

'Nobody locks their doors here,' Ivor said with a shocked expression on his face. 'What would they want to do that for?'

Mrs Grant paused on the threshold and looked at the boy with approval. 'You're quite right, young man. We are going to get on well, you and I.'

Ivor nodded in a matter-of-fact way. 'I'll get the other bags,' he said, running down the path and meeting Martin half way. 'Here! I'll take those,' he insisted, determined to finish the job he had begun.

With the sun pouring down on her upturned face, Claire stood listening to a lark singing high in the clear blue sky. There was a tight feeling in her throat. It was almost too perfect.

Martin was at her side, listening too,

waving as Ivor departed pulling the trolley down the rough country lane.

'Let's look around,' he said, taking Claire's hand.

Bending his head under the low porch, he held the door open, following her into the living room where Mrs Grant was rocking herself slowly in the chair at the side of the big open fireplace.

Claire continued through to the kitchen with its blackleaded range and auxiliary paraffin stove, and the one cold tap above the shallow stone sink. She could hear Blodwen's footsteps on the floor above and returned to the living room in time to see her coming down the bare wooden staircase which opened off a corner of the room.

'Just like the old days,' Blodwen said. 'No electric or water.'

'There's a cold tap in the kitchen,' Claire said, already loving the little house, sensitive to the implied slight.

'The electricity will have to wait until the war is over,' Martin said apologetically. 'It's all a bit primitive I'm afraid. I never gave it a thought. I should have warned you.'

'There's nothing wrong with the simple life,' Mrs Grant said firmly, getting to her feet.

'Don't think I'm grumbling,' Blodwen

said, with a pensive smile. 'It reminds me of when I was a girl.'

Martin took Mrs Grant's arm. 'You must have first choice of bedroom,' he said, and followed her up the narrow staircase.

'They don't waste any space in these cottages,' she observed as she peered through the open doors leading off the small landing. 'Yes . . . I think Blodwen and I should have these adjoining rooms,' she added. 'Then, if you have the room at that end . . . ' She indicated the isolated room at the right-hand side of the staircase. 'Claire can be at this end.'

'We're very well chaperoned,' he said with a wry twist of the mouth.

They had finished unpacking and Blodwen, accepting Claire's help without too much protest, was organizing a simple meal when there was a loud knock on the front door. Martin opened the door to find Ivor outside, a small bowl in his hand.

'Auntie Gwyneth sent these for your breakfast,' he said.

Martin looked down at the four speckled brown eggs. 'Well, that is kind of her,' he said, reaching into his pocket. 'Come in, Ivor.'

'They're a present,' Ivor said hastily, and Martin took a handkerchief from his pocket, as though the thought of payment had never entered his head.

'New laid eggs!' They could have been pure gold judging from Blodwen's delighted expression. And when the boy returned home she stood at the window watching him go. 'There's still some kindness left in the world,' she said with a sigh.

'You can say that again.' Martin gave her a hug. 'I saw you putting the last of your month's sweet ration in his pocket.'

'Get on with you,' she said, digging him in the ribs. 'Poor lad. Motherless, he is . . . and his father thousands of miles away. I go to chapel on Sunday, but I see something like that and I wonder . . . why?' She turned a perplexed face to Martin.

'Perhaps to give the Auntie Gwyneths of this world a chance to shine.'

'A funny old world,' she said, shaking her head and turning her attention to the smoking oil stove.

Mrs Grant and Blodwen went early to bed. They had little stamina and the change of air had made them sleepy.

'Still like the middle of the day,' Martin said, glancing at his watch. 'Getting on for ten o'clock. Double Summer Time has its limitations. How can I whisper sweet nothings in your ear without a big yellow

61

moon and at least a sprinkling of stars?'

Claire laughed, and yet she was not entirely at ease. There was something brittle about their relationship. Was it possible that they might never again return to the relaxed nonchalance of the past?

'I wonder if we can get down to the sea,' she said, standing on tip-toe to look over the hedge. 'Let's try before it gets dark.'

They strolled along the winding lane, past the station, to the footbridge spanning the track. Half way across the bridge they were met by a khaki-clad figure.

'You going somewhere?' he said, leaning against the wooden handrail, his fist around the barrel of his rifle.

'Down to the sea, if we can get there,' Martin said.

'Daytime, yes,' the man said. 'But the Home Guard patrol at night.' He jerked his thumb towards the sea. 'Darkness plays tricks with the imagination. We can get a bit trigger-happy if we see something that shouldn't be there.'

'Don't take a pot shot at us for the next half hour. Okay?'

With a wink, the man nodded his head towards the sea.

'Don't go beyond the wall,' he called after them.

The sun, dipping beneath the waves, spread the last of its light across the water. Threading up the shingle the incoming tide lapped the sea wall, dragging back in a whisper of tossed pebbles. There was no other soul in sight. The Home Guard had retreated for a quiet smoke before beginning his patrol.

Resting her elbows on the sea wall and cupping her chin in her hands, Claire said, 'It's so peaceful. Who would think there was a war on?'

Even the blockhouse on the promontory and the embroidery of barbed wire faded into insignificance before the quiet power of the sun and sea.

As the sun disappeared below the horizon a light breeze shivered across the waves. Claire shivered with it — a reflex action more than a feeling of cold. Martin's arm tightened around her shoulders, drawing her close.

She turned in his encircling arms to face him. Time rocked on its heels. No yesterday. No tomorrow. Only now.

Their lips met, touching gently, once, twice. For one fleeting moment Claire marvelled at the metamorphosis: childhood companions — enemies at worst; friends; now . . . ? But again his lips claimed hers, this time with an urgency which was echoed in her own response.

Martin held her then at arm's length.

'Where have you been hiding all these years?' he murmured, the incredulity in his eyes heightening her own delight.

Even heavy boots on the bridge could not dispel the magic.

'It's time to go,' Martin said, brushing his lips against her cheek. 'I won't risk you getting shot . . . not now.'

They called 'Goodnight' to the guard and slowly, unwilling to risk losing the elusive enchantment of that moment, returned to the cottage.

The pale streak of light beneath Mrs Grant's door told them that she was awaiting their return. Reluctantly, Martin left Claire at her bedroom door.

It took her a long time to get to sleep that night. At first so remote from the cottage, the war edged in, impossible to ignore: the unknown, forcing the feelings of elation into sharper focus, yet tinging them with a shadow of dread.

In the morning, Martin was already in the garden when Claire put her head out of the bedroom window.

'Couldn't you sleep?' she called.

He left the loaded wheelbarrow where it was and strolled over to the window, looking up at her with a half smile. 'Well, could you?' he asked.

She shook her head, feeling the colour come to her cheeks.

'Come and have a swim before breakfast,' he said. 'I've already checked. It's safe to get in just beyond the end of the sea wall. The tide's coming in. Best time of the day.'

'Five minutes,' Claire said.

'Two,' he insisted, running for the door.

Claire slipped into her swim-suit and tucking her feet into her sandals, grabbed a towel and raced down the stairs.

'Back in ten minutes,' she called to Blodwen who was at the kitchen door, hands on her hips and a broad smile on her face.

Claire was already at the garden gate when Martin caught up with her. Laughing like excited children they ran to the beach, discarding their sandals and picking their way over the moving stones to the water's edge. Claire shrieked as the icy foam lapped her ankles, and shrieked louder as Martin swept her off her feet and carried her, gasping as the water deepened, with a final plunge into the embrace of the Irish Sea.

'Remember how we used to do this from home,' she said when they clambered at last from the tumbling waves.

'And you were a giggling schoolgirl.'

'I never giggled,' she said indignantly. 'It was all jazz and motor racing for you in those days. You'd never talk about anything else.'

'A slow developer, I suppose.' He grinned, ensnaring her in the damp folds of his towel, kissing the curve of her neck.

'Making up for lost time,' she said, before his lips effectively silenced her.

'Do you think we'll remember this day when we're very old?' he said, pulling her yet closer so that she felt the hard-muscled body, the strength . . . and the tenderness.

The sun went behind a cloud and Claire shivered.

Martin held her against his heart. She could hear the strong beat.

'When we're old,' he said, 'I'll bring you back and remind you of today.'

'I'll keep you to that,' she said solemnly, her eyes looking deep into his.

'You're getting cold.' He slapped her lightly on the bottom. 'Race you back for breakfast.'

She wondered if he too felt the chill which had enveloped her and had little to do with the capricious sun.

5

As Claire dressed, her mind kept returning to the pre-war days when they used to have parties on the beach near the red and yellow sandstone caves. Always in the summer there was one really big party. Martin had told her that she would remember the good times. She smiled to herself. July . . . the party would have been on his birthday.

She went into her grandmother's room and speaking quietly, said, 'D'you realize that Saturday will be Martin's twenty-first?'

'His coming of age? I'd no idea. We must have some sort of celebration, of course. I wish I'd known before. We could have saved some of our rations.'

'Perhaps we'll be able to get . . . one or two extras,' Claire said tentatively.

'Not Black Market.' There was a warning glint in her grandmother's eyes. 'Blodwen and I can do little enough to help the war effort, but neither of us would countenance dealings which might hinder it, however minimally.'

'I wasn't planning an orgy,' Claire protested. 'I thought I might try to get a chicken.' She pulled a long face. 'I suppose we'll be lucky to get an old boiler. Not likely to get much else these days, but I'm sure Blodwen could do something with it. It won't be much of a party. We don't know anyone around here.'

'Just four of us,' Mrs. Grant said throwing up her hands in a gesture of frustration.

'And Ivor,' Claire said lamely. 'And his Auntie Gwyneth, and his uncle . . . if there is one. Not exactly riotous, but better than letting it slide past unnoticed. You'd think his father would have remembered.'

'Men are seldom much good at remembering anniversaries.'

Footsteps on the stairs and a knock at the door stopped further discussion. It was Martin with Mrs Grant's breakfast tray.

Claire took her chance to hurry down to explain the position to Blodwen, and between them they managed to get Martin to help with the washing-up after breakfast, while Claire picked up a shopping basket and took the short cut across the field to the station.

'Good morning,' she called to the Station Master who was checking some goods piled on a trolley. 'I'm looking for Ivor and his aunt. Do they live near here?'

Dragging the trolley to the swing gate between the platform and the garden, he beckoned to her to follow.

'Here, Gwyneth,' he called. 'The young lady wants to talk to you.'

'She's your wife?' Claire said.

He nodded, and Claire felt suddenly embarrassed. It was so odd to be asking three complete strangers to a birthday party. There was no time for preliminaries; there was nothing for it but to plunge straight in.

'We're having a bit of a party at lunchtime on Saturday, and we wondered if you and your husband and Ivor would come along?'

'Something special, is it?'

Claire explained, and asked if there was a farm where she might be able to buy a chicken.

'Jones, the farmer, would let her have a couple of boilers,' the Station Master said to his wife. 'He's coming down to pick up some stuff this afternoon.' He touched his nose and winked at Claire. 'Don't you worry,' he said. 'I'll have a word with him.'

'My husband won't be able to get away from his work,' the woman said, 'but me and Ivor, we'd love to come.'

'We're keeping it a secret,' Claire said. 'We'll look forward to seeing you on Saturday, Mrs . . . ?' She had almost called the woman Auntie Gwyneth.

'Williams,' the woman said. 'And I'll have a word with Annie along at the shop. If she

69

has any little extras under the counter, she'll slip you something.'

'You've been so kind already,' Claire said. 'Those eggs were such a treat.'

'I'll let you have a few more before Saturday.'

'Oh, please . . . no!' Claire said. 'We couldn't take them.'

It had seemed ungrateful not to mention the eggs, but now she was afraid that her thanks might have appeared like a feeler for more, and wished she had said nothing.

Mrs Williams waved away her embarrassment. 'There!' she said. 'I want you to have them.' Her round face glowed. It was easy to see why Ivor spoke of his Auntie Gwyneth with such warmth.

The arrangements went ahead. Blodwen did her cooking when Claire and Martin went further afield, exploring the hills and coastline. It was on one of these days that Claire found the present she was going to give to Martin: a small oil painting of a limewashed cottage. It could have been the White Cottage itself. While he was enquiring about buses she bought the painting and hid it in her shoulder-bag.

★ ★ ★

70

On the Saturday morning Martin was the last one down to breakfast, and even he was early.

'Happy Birthday to you!' the chorus greeted him.

'How did you know?' A smile spread over his face.

'Our first swim reminded me of the parties we used to have,' Claire said. 'I didn't have much opportunity to search for a present.' She handed him the small parcel. 'I hope you like it.'

He removed the paper and held the picture up to the light. For a few moments he said nothing. Then, putting it down carefully on the table, he took her in his arms. 'You're a genius,' he said, kissing her again, and again.

They forgot that they were not alone until Mrs Grant's short cough acted as a reminder. She handed Martin a gold hunter which had belonged to her husband. 'It still keeps good time,' she said, as though it was just any old watch, but he knew that it was very much more than that — more than a present, a sign of approval.

Martin had several unexpected gifts that day. From Blodwen came a silver pocket-knife in exchange for a ha'penny, which she had insisted on extracting for fear of cutting their friendship. From Ivor, there was a piece of driftwood rubbed smooth, and polished, looking like a seagull in flight. Mr Williams had supplied some of his own plum cordial for the toast, and his wife had produced a long, Air Force blue scarf.

'I wish your father could have been here,' Mrs Grant said when Ivor and his aunt had gone home.

'He tried to get his leave for this week,' Martin said, 'but he's in the United States at the moment, unless his orders have been changed. He never was one for parties anyway. I'm very touched that you took so much trouble. Just let me bring in Father's contribution.'

He went through to the kitchen and they could hear him opening the pantry door. He came back with four glasses, and a bottle of Champagne which had been chilled in a bucket of cold water.

'I couldn't produce this while Mrs Williams was here. Her husband's plum cordial had to take pride of place.'

Mrs Grant agreed, but her lips were a little twitchy at the memory of the sharp concoction.

'Not really chilled enough,' Martin said, as he eased the cork out.

Despite all his efforts, the cork shot across

the room and the wine threatened to follow it.

Claire and he, between them, holding the glasses to catch the effervescence, managed to save most of it, and it put a shine on their celebrations.

★ ★ ★

Too soon it was their last full day. Walking along the coast, Claire and Martin stopped to sit on a grassy slope overlooking the sea. The sun, reaching down to the rocks beneath the surface of the water, revealed pools of vibrant colour: blue — as dark as the night sky, aquamarine, green and amber.

'Who would believe it could be so beautiful?' Claire said, watching the colours change and blend.

'There's a lot I find hard to believe,' Martin said. 'Some things I'll never understand . . . like . . . when did you stop being just the brat next door?'

She turned her face to his, laughing. But he was not laughing.

'God! I love you, Claire.' His voice was almost fierce. 'Will you wait for me until this war is over?'

It was like a slap in the face.

Stunned, Claire wondered what she had

73

expected him to say. After the war. That seemed far away in the future: something to yearn for, but vague, obscure.

'I love you,' he said again. 'When I met you at Lime Street on your last leave, I think I knew it then.'

She looked away, unwilling to allow him to see how his words had stung her.

'You haven't answered my question,' he said.

To Claire, falling in love meant wedding bells and all the trimmings. She knew there could be no wedding bells now that their use was reserved as a warning of invasion. No wedding bells, but why no wedding?

'We love each other,' she said, trying to get things straight in her own mind. 'Why wait? Is it that you're not sure?' She paused, forcing herself to look at him, to see the truth in his eyes. 'Or, is it just the spell of the White Cottage?'

'Call it a spell if you like,' he said, tilting her chin as she tried to look away, 'but I want you more than I've ever wanted anything — anybody — in all my life.'

'But next year, or the year after that, or . . .'

'Don't you understand?' He spoke slowly, as though every word was agony. 'A wife and a widow almost in the same breath.

Oh, Claire! I've seen it happen too often.'

'And do you think I don't know the risks?' There were tears in her eyes.

'We'd want a family, wouldn't we?'

She nodded.

'It's no world for bringing up a child . . . especially on your own.'

'The war!' Her voice was bitter. 'It's like a spider's web. We can't escape it, even here.'

A dog ran past and a group of children followed, running and tumbling down the slope.

Martin stood up, pulling Claire to her feet.

'It won't last forever,' he said, kissing her gently on the lips.

They walked back along the coast road and found Ivor waiting at the cottage to arrange about the collection of luggage the following day.

'You asked her to marry you yet?' he said, looking at them with his head on one side.

'I've told you before,' Martin said, ruffling the boy's hair and brandishing a fist under his nose. 'Mind your own business.'

'Auntie Gwyneth saw it in the tealeaves.' He looked worried. 'Someone else, is it?'

'No one else.'

'That's all right then.' He pulled his socks

up. 'Ask her now. Go on!'

But Claire had already run into the house, and from her room she could hear Ivor's voice: 'There!' he said impatiently. 'You've missed your chance.'

'You tell your Auntie Gwyneth her tealeaves were jumping the gun, looking into the future when the war is over.'

'There's stupid!' Ivor turned his head towards the house. 'Won't she marry you till then?'

'I won't ask her until then.'

'Why?'

'You ask too many questions.'

'You think you might get killed?' Ivor said, with a child's uncomplicated view coming straight to the point.

From her window, Claire watched Martin's face. She wished they had not stirred up the cold facts which they lived with every day but tried so hard to ignore.

'I've told you before,' Martin said. 'You ask too many questions.'

Ivor shrugged, and then remembered what he had come about in the first place. 'I'll have to take the bags down first thing in the morning,' he said. 'I'm helping on the farm in the holidays, and Mr Jones wants me there early tomorrow.'

'They'll be ready,' Martin said.

6

Claire's arrival back at camp coincided with Edna's departure.

'What sort of course is it?' Claire said, helping her friend with her packing.

Edna shrugged. 'Haven't a clue. Very hush-hush. And I hear you've definitely applied for a posting nearer home.'

'The grapevine doesn't miss a trick, does it?'

'The Queen Bee is on your side. She's been in contact with Group already. Let me have your home address. I'd like to keep in touch.'

Within a month, Claire was packing her own kit.

Waiting at the Guard Room for a lift to the station, she could see 'C' Crew getting into the truck to go up to the technical site. She waved to them all . . . people she knew so well and might never see again. She felt that she was leaving a small piece of herself behind.

Preslan? Claire wondered why her new posting sounded vaguely familiar. As the slow train pulled out of Chester she realized that it was the same line which had taken her to the White Cottage only weeks before.

She expected to find the Waafery in a hutted camp on the hills behind the town, and was surprised to discover that she would be living in a hostel not far from the railway station, in what had been a private hotel before the war.

The front door of the hostel was open. She crossed the glass-covered verandah to the hall, which overlooked a stretch of lawn where a small group of girls lay on the grass, sunbathing.

'I didn't hear you arrive.'

Claire turned to see a WAAF sergeant coming from the passage beside the staircase.

'LACW Grant,' Claire said. 'Posted from Danborough.'

'My name's Miller,' the sergeant said with a welcoming smile. 'Normally known — as if you couldn't guess — as Dusty. I'm in charge here. You've had quite a journey. I suppose you came via Wing HQ?' Without waiting for a reply she picked Claire's kitbag off the floor and, tucking it under her arm as if it were a bundle of feathers, started up the stairs. 'Come on. I'll show you your room.'

Dusty was another Edna. Claire had no objection to being taken under her wing, especially as she felt fit to drop.

Informality appeared to be the watchword, but there was no sign of slackness about the hostel. The furniture was polished until it shone, there was no vestige of clutter, and yet there was a warm, homely feeling about the place.

'You'll share with Janet,' Dusty said, dropping the kitbag and opening the door into a small room with a window giving a view of the kitchen garden. 'You'll be on the same watch. They're on one to six today. If you'd like to eat with them when they come off duty, it will give you time to freshen up.' She stepped outside, delving into a cupboard on the landing and reappearing with fresh linen.

'Three watch, or four?' Claire asked, opening her kitbag.

'Four, thank goodness,' Dusty said, pulling the 'biscuits' — the three-part mattress — along the bare bed springs. 'When you've made that up, come down to the kitchen for a mug of tea.'

By the time Claire had investigated the kitchen, had some tea, and taken a tepid bath, it was almost time for supper. She could hear the truck turning into the drive, and the clatter of feet on the uncarpeted stairs.

Janet Preston burst into the room and

slung her respirator and steel helmet into a corner. The two girls looked at each other in surprise.

'Where have we met before?' Claire said.

'Square bashing at Morecambe,' Janet said, and Claire remembered at once the diminutive blonde who could never sort out her left hand from her right, making a shambles of every parade, and yet always managing to get away with it.

'I'm coming on your watch,' Claire said, stifling a yawn. 'But, right now, I could do with a meal and a good sleep.'

At supper, Claire met the two other girls on the crew: Tina, whose parents could never have anticipated her ample form when they named her; and Jackie, the only married one amongst them.

It was not until the following morning that Claire met the complete crew.

After early breakfast she went outside where the truck was waiting.

'We pick up the men on the way. They're billeted in the town,' Janet explained, hitting the side of the truck to let the driver know that they were all aboard. He secured the tailboard and drove to the far end of the town.

'Claire, meet Danny and Bob,' Janet said as two bleary-eyed airmen climbed aboard.

'Where are the others?'

'Walked up,' Danny grunted.

'Looks as though a walk might have done you good this morning,' Tina said, slapping him on the shoulder. 'Get off your knees, Danny boy!'

'If you've *got* to speak, do it *quietly*,' Danny said, holding his head, and almost losing his balance as the truck lurched forward, labouring up the steep hill out of the town where the road narrowed to a single track. They continued in silence until the truck pulled into a lay-by beside a cluster of cottages and the driver got out to collect a can of milk.

'Press on regardless,' Danny said with a groan as the engine restarted.

Bob remained silent, huddled in the corner of the truck, his eyes closed.

There was barely enough room for the wheels to clear the overgrown banks at either side. There was little to see, but at last they reached the Guard Room flanked by high barbed wire.

It was not until they left the truck and walked over the brow of the hill that Claire caught her first glimpse of the rectangular, box-shaped aerial, swinging in an arc, scanning sky and sea.

The short walk to the operations block

revived the two men, and Claire was already losing the feeling of strangeness as she waited with the rest of the crew for the door to be opened.

Inside, the layout was reasonably familiar, with the exception of the cathode ray tube. Here, instead of the flickering horizontal trace, the beam of light — like the radius of a circle — swept the face of the tube, leaving a bright impression of the coastline with shipping and aircraft showing as streaks of light, tiny crescent shapes moving with each sweep of the beam. The tube was marked with a grid so that the map references could be read after each scanning.

Claire quickly settled into the new routine: a calmer order of things, with only an occasional hint of enemy activity, but with always the same careful watch. It was more difficult to keep alert without the adrenaline-boosting action of the hostile attack, without even the diversion of the enemy meteorological aircraft, Weather Willie. It seemed odd to Claire that the bombers which had destroyed her home would have been tracked in that room.

On Friday morning Claire left the hostel after late breakfast and was home before lunch. It was reassuring to know that she could get there so quickly, and Blodwen was overjoyed to see her.

'Your grandmother is in bed for a few days,' she said. 'No, don't go up yet.' She put a hand on Claire's arm. 'I want to talk to you first.'

'What's wrong?'

'Nothing alarming. She had a bit of a turn last Sunday. Her heart. The doctor says it's the effect of the 'flu. He says she should be quite all right if she takes it quietly until she can build up her strength again. That little holiday did her a lot of good, but you know what she's like, the moment she feels better she thinks she can push a wall over.'

'I sometimes forget that she's getting old.'

Claire crept upstairs expecting to find her grandmother asleep, but Mrs Grant was sitting up in bed reading the newspaper.

'Claire!' She put down the paper and pointed towards the open window and to the distant view of the Welsh hills. 'Look at that! You're so near, we can almost see you from here.'

'You old fraud!' Claire said. 'I expected to see you pale and wan, and here you are . . .'

'Fit as a flea,' the old lady said, putting up her face to be kissed. 'No need to keep me in bed like this.'

'Oh, yes there is. I should have thought

last Sunday would have told you that.'

'Blodwen's been talking, has she?'

'She should have let me know at once.'

'Are you happy, Claire?' Mrs Grant swiftly changed the subject away from her own health. 'Have you seen Martin recently?'

'Is one dependent on the other?' Claire asked, laughing.

'Only you can tell me that.'

'He wants me to marry him,' Claire said, wondering how much her grandmother knew or guessed, 'but not until after the war.' She walked over to the window, afraid to show the confusion of her own private limbo.

'Yes. He asked my permission.'

'He . . . ?' Claire turned, the smile of her face a mixture of surprise, joy, relief, and a hint of something deeper. 'He did, did he? Well, he must be serious . . . '

'You doubted it?'

Claire could not answer at once, and when she did her voice was hesitant: 'No . . . not really,' she said.

'That means you did.'

'Not in the way you imagine,' Claire said. 'It all happened so quickly.' She shook her head, frowning. 'No, that's not entirely true. How can I explain? That week at the cottage — we were on another planet.'

'I understand.'

'I wish I did.'

'Give it time, child.'

'Time may be the one thing we haven't got.'

If Claire had expected reassuring platitudes she would have been disappointed, but she knew her grandmother too well for that.

'Life is no neat little plan,' the old lady said firmly. 'And that applies to each and every one of us from the day we're born. A tangle. A labyrinth. We fight our way through as best we can.'

'You're a comfort, I must say.'

'It has its good side too. You were happy on your last leave.'

'But, is he right?' Claire said. 'Should we wait until after the war? Oh damn! Damn! Damn! I shouldn't be bothering you with this.'

'Indeed you should not!' It was Blodwen coming into the room with a tray of coffee. 'And such language!'

'If you must listen at keyholes, you must expect to be shocked occasionally,' Mrs Grant said sharply.

Claire had only one night at home, but it was long enough to convince her that Martin had been right to encourage the move.

It was only a few days later that Martin arrived unexpectedly at the hostel.

'There's an air crew type asking for you,' Janet said. 'You'd better get your skates on, or there'll be a stampede!'

Claire ran down the stairs straight into Martin's arms.

'Come to the cottage with me,' he said. 'We can get some lunch on the way. I don't have to get back until the morning.'

She hesitated for a moment, and Martin laughed. 'It's all right,' he said. 'I haven't got designs on you ... well, yes, I have ... but I'd have to answer to your grandmother. That sort of trouble I can do without.' He kissed her lips and the tip of her nose. 'Cross my heart, I'll bring you back before twenty-three fifty-nine.'

It was early afternoon when they walked across the field to the cottage.

'Ivor's doing his job,' Martin said approvingly as they walked up the path. 'We have an arrangement about the garden.'

Claire went inside, opening the windows and letting the warm breeze blow through. She was struggling with one of the catches when Martin took her by the shoulders and turned her to face him.

'I haven't changed my mind about wartime weddings,' he said, 'but I must know. Have you made up your mind? Will you marry me when it's all over?'

'I'd marry you tomorrow,' Claire said softly, 'but if that's the way it has to be, I'll wait for you.'

'I want everything to be right for you, Claire. We'll grow old together. Here, maybe.'

'Living on fresh air, I suppose?'

For a moment his face clouded. 'You're right. I don't even know if I'll be able to support a wife.'

'What will you do for a living?'

'Teach, perhaps.'

He took a small blue leather box from his pocket. 'I'm not sure whether you'll like this,' he said. 'You don't have to have it if . . .'

'Well, show me,' Claire cut in impatiently.

He took out a sapphire ring in an old-fashioned setting.

'But, it's beautiful!' Claire gasped.

'It was my grandmother's. You don't mind?' he said anxiously.

'Mind? What a crazy thing to ask.'

'I wondered if you might prefer a new one.'

'We'd never find one as unique and lovely as this.'

Martin slid the ring onto her finger. 'Now I can face Ivor,' he said with a grin.

'Oh, is that the only reason?' As she spoke,

the garden gate slammed shut. Through the open window they could see Ivor plodding up the path.

He knocked and, without waiting for an answer, opened the door and came in. Immediately his face lit up as he saw the ring on Claire's finger.

'Auntie Gwyneth was right then,' he said with satisfaction. 'About time too!'

'I'm glad you approve,' Martin said, lifting Claire's hand for his inspection.

They were summoned to the station house for tea and congratulations and only with difficulty got away in time to snatch a light meal and get Claire back to the hostel.

'I wish I was going back to the cottage with you,' Claire said when she had to leave Martin at the hostel door.

'Hussy!' he said, kissing her with a passion which left her breathless and alight. 'I think Auntie Gwyneth knew what she was doing, keeping us away from the cottage. She had me weighed up. I wouldn't mind betting she sent Ivor along as soon as she saw us crossing the field.' He chuckled. 'Next time we'll take the bus.'

'When will I see you again?'

'Soon,' he said.

'And Auntie Gwyneth needn't worry. I'd always be safe with you.'

'I don't know that I'd count on that too much if I were you,' he said, ruffling her hair, kissing her until she gasped for breath, murmuring her name like an incantation.

A jangle of keys told them that the hostel was about to be locked for the night.

'I must go,' Claire whispered. 'Come again soon, Martin . . . very soon.' She paused on the step. 'And . . . take care.'

She stood on the verandah and watched him go with a mixture of joy and fear, one emotion heightening the other until she felt torn apart.

Janet was asleep by the time Claire got up to their room, but the following morning she was the first to see the sapphire ring.

'Claire! You're engaged!'

It was only minutes before the hostel was alive with the news, and the questions came thick and fast.

'When's the wedding?'

'Where's he stationed?'

'Is he on op's?'

Claire put her hands to her head and wailed for peace. 'One at a time,' she begged.

'When's the wedding? That's what we want to know,' Tina said.

'After the war.'

The silence that followed her words was

accentuated by the furore which had gone on before.

'You're . . . not serious?' Tina said hesitantly, laughing nervously to cover her embarrassment.

Claire nodded.

'You'll change your minds,' Jackie said confidently.

'And she should know,' Tina said.

'Yes,' Jackie said. 'Bill had the same idea, but not for long. Took him about three weeks to change his mind.'

'Does your grandmother know?' Dusty asked.

'Not yet.'

'You can ring her from here if you like.'

'Thanks, Dusty. I'm going to see her at the weekend. I'll save it until then.'

When Claire got home later that week her grandmother and Blodwen showed no great surprise, but beneath their happiness she sensed a feeling of anxiety. She recognized it because she felt it herself. Despite the even tenor of life at Preslan, she was living on a knife edge.

★ ★ ★

And then the summer was gone in a series of brief reunions and abortive meetings;

arrangements made and un-made; duty always having to come first. The autumn of 1943; the Italians had surrendered to the Allies; the Germans had bombed Rome and were having a tough time on the Russian front. Into the fifth year of war.

Claire's promotion had just come through. She was sewing on her corporal's tapes when Janet came upstairs to find her.

'There's someone asking for you down in the hall,' she said, and Claire was off her bed, through the door, and half way down the stairs before Janet could draw breath.

'Martin!'

But even as the word left her lips she knew it was not Martin standing there looking into the garden. It was Roy Baldwin. She had not seen him since their school days, but there was no mistaking the rugged features. But where was that cocky tilt of the chin and the over-confident stance?

'Claire . . .'

She could tell from the awkward way he approached her that there was bad news.

'Is it . . . Martin?'

He nodded. 'I'm sorry, Claire. He bought it over France.' His mouth contorted into a hard line and there was a pause before he could continue. 'It was a shambles. They threw everything at us.'

This was the moment she had been half-expecting for so long. She had almost rehearsed it, preparing herself for the tears and the pain. But there was no pain. She stood before him dry-eyed, feeling nothing.

'You've come a long way,' she said, looking at her watch. 'It's a bit early for lunch, but I'm sure . . . '

He put a hand on her arm. No stranger to the varying reactions to bad news, he was not shocked by her apparent indifference.

'We'll probably go out again tonight. I shouldn't be here now, but Martin wanted me to let you know if . . . anything happened. If we get any definite gen, I'll let you know at once.'

When he had gone, Claire stood in the hall for a long time staring into the garden. She made no move as Janet walked past.

'Are you all right, Claire?' Janet asked, turning back — although she knew the answer almost before the question left her lips.

Still, Claire made no move. She was twisting the ring on her finger, looking down at the deep blue stone. She was cold. The stone was all she could see. Blue. Deep blue.

Janet needed no telling. It was all there.

Claire swayed, her knees crumpled beneath her and she sank unconscious to the floor before her friend could reach her.

The following day she was kept in bed under the care of the Medical Officer, fussed over by Dusty. She still shed no tears.

'Is it 'C' Crew's day off tomorrow, Dusty?' Claire asked late that evening.

'Yes.'

'Will you let me go off for the day?'

'You're not fit to go home yet.'

'But, Dusty . . . '

'You stay here. And that's an order. If it's any help, I'll go and break the news to your grandmother . . . '

'It's good of you, but no. That's something I must do, but not just yet.' Claire looked away, trying not to visualize the faces of her grandmother and Blodwen when the news was broken.

The following morning when everyone was at breakfast, Claire crept out of the hostel. She needed solitude, and she knew she would get that at the cottage.

Mr Williams hailed her like an old friend. She was glad he was busy with a load of boxes. Taking her chance, she hurried off the platform, past the chapel and across the meadow.

At the cottage gate she paused. The first tears stung her eyes. Slowly she walked up the path, resting her head against the door as if begging for comfort. After a few moments she opened the door and stepped inside. Dropping into the rocking chair, all restraint gone, she wept.

Long after all the tears had dried she sat gazing into the empty grate. The watery sun slid behind the clouds, and the room felt cold and damp. Claire pulled her greatcoat around her legs, but there was no comfort in the stiff material. She shivered and got to her feet.

She had half expected to feel Martin's presence at the cottage, but she felt nothing. Ivor would soon be home from school. He would have to know the truth . . . but not before she could face it herself.

She went outside, closing the door behind her, and took the winding lane towards the station. There was plenty of time before the train was due. No need to take the short cut, to risk an early encounter with Ivor. The piercing wind bit into her flesh. She had eaten nothing since breakfast, and had touched little enough of that. She walked past the station, crossing the footbridge to the sea wall. The sea was grey and angry, crashing through the shingle, no gentle rhythm but a continuous pounding.

Claire was cold. So cold.

It was two hours later when Corporal Jones of the Home Guard almost tripped over her unconscious body.

7

It was two days before Claire surfaced again. Even then, she was barely aware of her surroundings; just vague impressions . . . her grandmother, Blodwen, Dusty, the nurses. Then, late one morning she awoke to find her mind clear. The pain of reality overwhelmed her and she shut her eyes, trying to return to oblivion. When she opened them again Dusty was looking down at her.

'Corporal Grant,' she said, wagging a finger at Claire and drawing up a chair to the bedside, 'I should put you on a charge.'

'I had to get away on my own.'

'And nearly died in the process.'

'That might have solved a lot of things.'

'I don't think your grandmother would agree with you there,' Dusty said sharply, getting up as the sister came into the side ward. 'You'll be going on sick leave when you are fit enough to travel. Now, I must go.'

'Thanks for coming, Dusty. I didn't . . . I didn't do it on purpose, you know.'

Dusty turned back and touched Claire's

hand in a simple gesture of sympathy. 'I know,' she said, and hurried away.

Dusty had only been gone a few minutes, and the sister was checking Claire's pulse, when footsteps and voices outside the door interrupted the calm of the hospital routine. An RAF padre put his head around the door, and asked, 'May I see your patient, Sister?'

The sister joined him in the corridor, closing the door behind her. The ensuing conversation was lost to Claire who wondered whether to feign sleep. She wanted no uplifting words of comfort.

The door opened again.

'Do you feel strong enough to cope with some good news?'

Without moving, Claire opened her eyes.

'I didn't think you were asleep,' the padre said with a smile. 'It is good news, I promise you.' Patiently he waited for her to grasp the implication of his words.

'Is he a prisoner of war?' Her voice was little more than a whisper.

'Better than that.' He paused, knowing that she was still weak. 'He's here, waiting to see you.'

The message took a few moments to penetrate.

'Martin . . . here?'

And then, there he was, standing in the doorway.

The padre left, unnoticed.

Claire and Martin were locked in each other's arms; neither spoke nor moved for what seemed an eternity. At last, Claire lay back on the pillow. She tried to speak, but the words would not come. Tentatively, she put her hand out to touch Martin's face as though unable to believe that he was really there.

'Claire . . . Claire.' His arms enfolded her again, his lips buried in her hair, lank now from days of fever.

The door opened.

'You must leave now,' the sister said, not without sympathy.

'Oh! But, Sister!' Claire protested, finding her voice again. 'Just a few minutes . . . *please*.'

The sister's stern expression relaxed a little and, smiling, she tipped up the watch pinned to her uniform. 'Two minutes more,' she said crisply, closing the door.

'How . . . ?' Claire's voice choked in her throat.

'We were lucky,' Martin said. 'We went down off the coast and were picked up by some fishermen. They risked everything to get us back. I'd sooner have my job than theirs.'

'How long have you been back?'

'I came as soon as I could,' he said, and she knew he had given her all the information she would get. An unguarded word in the wrong ear could mean disaster to friends on the other side of the Channel. He was back. That was all that mattered.

'I felt so alone,' she said.

'Proves my point. Wartime marriages are a mistake.' His voice held less conviction than before.

'As your wife, I would have felt a part of it all. Involved. Instead . . . ' She bit her lip, fighting back the stinging tears. 'Instead, I was on the outside. Like a stranger.'

'They told me you were found on the sea wall.'

'I had to get away.'

'You chose to be alone?' He was puzzled.

'I wanted to be somewhere where we'd been together . . . and happy. But, even at the cottage, you'd left no trace.'

The door burst open and the sister bustled in.

'You can come in this evening,' she said, dismissing Martin and beckoning to one of the nurses in the corridor. 'Rounds start any moment now. This bed is a disgrace!'

'I can't get back this evening,' Martin said. 'I have to return to my squadron.'

'I'm sorry about that, but Matron is always on time.'

'Damn Matron,' he said under his breath and taking Claire into his arms, once more made nonsense of the straightened covers.

'When will I see you again?' Claire called as he was hustled from the room.

'As soon as I can make it,' he said, forcing his head around the door. 'I have to report back tonight. I'll go and see your grandmother now. She's staying at the cottage until . . . '

But the rest of the sentence was lost as the door was flung wide and Matron with attendant retinue swept in.

After the shock of Martin's return, Claire sank back into a deep sleep, awakening in the late afternoon.

'The very last roses of the summer,' the nurse said, poking a thermometer under Claire's tongue, and breathing a prolonged sigh. 'No one ever sent me twelve red roses. Not even in peacetime.'

Claire picked up the small envelope from her locker and read the few words on the enclosed card over and over again.

'Does he love you, then?' the nurse asked archly, removing the thermometer and craning her neck in an attempt to read the card, which said, briefly and to the point:

'Darling Claire,
Will you marry me at the
end of this tour of op's?
    All my love,
        Martin'

'I rather think he does,' Claire said.

8

The wedding was all set for late November; it was to take place on Claire's twentieth birthday.

Back at Preslan, fully recovered, she counted the weeks, the days, the minutes. Although determined never again to anticipate disaster, she found it impossible to dismiss its shadow entirely from her mind, and so the relief when Martin rang to say that the tour was completed was almost overwhelming.

That evening, on watch, Claire was bubbling over with the news.

'I can't believe it. I thought that last tour would never end,' she said when she and Janet were brewing up towards the end of their spell of duty.

'The war's not over yet, you know,' Danny called, the chinagraph pencil dangling from his fingers as he finished doodling on one corner of the perspex-covered map.

'Take no notice of him. He's cheesed off because the barmaid at the local is joining the Land Army,' one of the mechanics said, picking up two of the mugs. 'I say a celebration is called for.'

'Yes. I'm going to be married next week.' Claire pushed a mug of tea into Danny's hand. 'Smile, darn you . . . smile!'

Her high spirits were infectious and the following evening the hostel was en fête for a 'shaky do'. The party went on until the early hours – a dispensation on the part of Dusty who took her responsibilities seriously, even though with a light hand.

The following morning there was all the clearing-up to be done. Dressed in overalls, Claire was wielding a duster in the large rest room when Dusty opened the door.

'Corporal,' she said stiffly. 'Will you come into my office, please.'

Claire could see the CO's car outside in the drive. That accounted for the formal approach.

'Right. I'll just finish this table,' Claire said, crawling underneath to make a good job of it.

'*Now*, Claire.' There was a hint of pleading in the sergeant's voice.

Claire slid out and got to her feet. 'What's up?' she said, but Dusty had already gone.

Perhaps the CO had had a complaint about the party. Claire groaned inwardly. She was in no mood to be downtrodden. Everything was right with her world. She had not been told to change so, still clutching her duster, she went into the office.

It was more than a reprimand for a noisy evening. She knew that the moment she crossed the threshold.

The CO addressed the wall above her head.

'I'm afraid I have bad news for you,' he said, and Claire's immediate thought was for her grandmother, until he continued: 'Flight Lieutenant Turner has been killed . . . '

'No!' Claire said emphatically. 'It can't be true. There's some mistake. He's not flying . . . '

'It was a road accident,' the CO said quietly. 'Fog, and the blackout.' He looked down, studying his shoes. 'If it's any comfort, it was instantaneous. He couldn't have felt anything.'

'A road accident?' She stood quite still, her face expressionless. 'Then . . . there can be no mistake?'

He shook his head slowly. 'I'm very sorry, Corporal. Please accept my sincere sympathy.'

★ ★ ★

Roy arrived later in the morning, this time a messenger without the consolation of hope: a role to which he was becoming uncomfortably accustomed. He knew the news had already been broken and was surprised to see Claire looking almost cheerful.

'Claire . . . ' He moved as though to put his arms around her for mutual comfort, but she turned away.

'I've shed my tears already . . . remember? Fate has played its little joke. It's funny when you think about it.'

'Stop it, Claire!' He gripped her arms. He had joked about death too often himself not to recognize it as a form of insulation, but there was a time for the hard-headed reaction, and this wasn't it. 'I've come to drive you home.' He paused. 'The funeral is on Friday.'

'Funeral?' She stared through him. She had given no thought to the formalities. 'An odd exchange for a wedding.' Her shoulders drooped, the facade was slipping. 'With that tour of op's over, I felt so sure that nothing could go wrong. The Germans couldn't do it. It had to be some fool behind the wheel of a car. Martin didn't believe in wartime weddings . . . not really. Well, there won't be any wedding now. I can't even wait for him until it's all over. It will never be over for me.'

'Go and pack what you'll need,' he said gently. 'I'll see if I can rustle up a warm drink. The fog is still thick, and there's no point in starting off cold.'

They were standing beside a long window overlooking the garden. Everything was shrouded in mist, the colours of autumn drained away.

'Take your time,' he said, putting his hands on her shoulders, trying to make some contact, to break through the barrier which could only cause more pain if it was allowed to remain.

'Time. That's the one thing I have got now,' she said, turning to face him. 'All the time in the world.'

Slowly, she went upstairs to pack. When she came down again Roy was drinking coffee with Dusty. He handed Claire a mug, stirring in some sugar.

'I don't take sugar,' she said, pulling a face.

'Drink it,' he insisted, and he watched until she drained the mug to its sludgy dregs.

'Take care of her.' Dusty's voice trembled with emotion. To Claire she could say nothing.

If anything, the fog had thickened. Claire turned up the collar of her coat, sinking down in the car seat, trying to keep out the piercing cold. Reality had slipped away.

She was hearing the CO's words over and over again, but those words were being spoken to someone else, not to her. It was as though a shutter had come down, isolating her from outside influences, leaving her glacially untouched.

Almost home, Roy put his foot on the brake, pulling into a lay-by.

'I don't know whether this is the time,' he said diffidently, 'but Martin asked me to give you a letter if anything happened to him.'

Reaching into his pocket he handed her an envelope and immediately started up the engine again.

'I'll look at it later,' she said vaguely.

'If there's anything I can do Claire . . . anything.'

'Thank you, Roy.' For just a moment his concern almost broke her iron control, but she regained her composure and spoke without any outward sign of emotion. 'You've done it already. All anyone could do.'

'I've been in touch with Martin's father, and four of us will be coming up for the funeral.' He drew a quick breath. 'I say! That's OK with you, I hope?'

'But, of course. D'you know where Colonel Turner is now?'

'He's staying with your grandmother.'

Arriving at the house, Roy made his

excuses and withdrew, going home to his parents.

Colonel Turner looked older. He bent to kiss Claire's cheek. His own control matched hers, touching her more deeply than any show of emotion might have done. But neither could accept an explosion of grief; both remained unnaturally calm, and the moment passed.

Mrs Grant sat very straight in her chair, pouring tea as though it needed every scrap of her concentration.

'Blodwen,' she said, lifting the lid of the hot water jug, 'I think we shall need a little more, don't you?'

'Yes, indeed,' Blodwen said, hurrying to the kitchen, moving things about as she waited for the kettle to boil, busy all the time — no opportunity for thought.

By the evening Claire was very tired, a feeling which was not to leave her even later in the week when the funeral was over and she was preparing to return to the hostel.

Her grandmother sat on the edge of Claire's bed watching her pack.

'My dear,' she said. 'I think you should apply to move from Preslan. You need a complete change.'

'I couldn't do that.'

'You can and you must. I'm stronger now,

and quite capable of standing on my own feet . . . with a little help from Blodwen.'

'But, Grandmother . . . '

'No buts.'

Further discussion was forestalled as Blodwen hurried into the room.

'It's Colonel Turner,' she said to Claire. 'He wants to see you before he goes back to London.'

Claire went downstairs into the drawing room where Martin's father stood with his back to her, gazing into the fire. Hearing her footsteps, he turned.

'Claire, my dear,' he said, 'there are one or two things I think we should discuss.'

Claire wondered what there was left to discuss.

'Martin was in the middle of settling his affairs with the wedding in view.' He paused, seeing her flinch at his words. With an embarrassed cough, he continued: 'He was making a Will, and the cottage, which I had already given to him, will be yours.'

'You said he was making a Will,' Claire said. 'Do you mean that it was not completed?'

He nodded.

'I don't want you to think I'm ungrateful,' she said at last. 'All I wanted was Martin. I don't need — don't want anything else.'

'Perhaps when you've had time to think it over, you'll change your mind.'

'I never want to see the cottage again.'

'No need to make a final decision now. Remember, it was Martin's wish, and I too would like you to have it, my dear. Your grandmother and Blodwen might care to go there occasionally for a few days.'

The matter was left in abeyance. When Claire returned to Preslan she thought she had seen the last of the White Cottage. In her pocket was Martin's letter, unopened, the final link which she was loth to sever.

Her name had been drawn to remain on duty over Christmas and so she did not apply for a posting at once. To go before the holiday might mean that one of the married men would be deprived of Christmas with his family.

She joined in the festivities with almost too much enthusiasm, her laughter too shrill, her energy inexhaustible. Even when she went home in the New Year the mask was never dropped; she became, if anything, more brittle.

'You wanted to know what I would like to do for my birthday next month,' her grandmother said.

'And you've decided?'

'I'd like a few days at the cottage. Blodwen

and I have an open invitation. Knowing how you feel, we wouldn't expect you to stay there, but come for the day . . . on my birthday.'

'Yes, of course.' Claire's voice was deceptively unconcerned.

When the day arrived she found it more difficult to maintain the cool exterior.

'You're going to the cottage?' Janet said, her face one big smile. 'I'm so glad. I thought perhaps . . . ' But her words faded at the sight of Claire's set smile. 'Oh, Claire! Can you . . . can you cope?'

'Of course I can cope.'

Claire picked up a small package from her locker, holding it tightly in her hand.

'You don't have to go,' Janet said.

'I wouldn't risk spoiling my grandmother's birthday.' Claire glanced at her watch. 'And I mustn't be late.'

She had made up her mind that this visit was to be no echo of the past and so, avoiding the railway station, she took the bus along the coast road. The nearest stop was about a mile from the cottage and it was not until the little house came into view that she allowed herself even to think about it.

At the first sight she wanted to turn and run. Had it been any other day, nothing would have persuaded her to take another step. With a deep breath, she squared her shoulders against the bite of the February wind and hurried the rest of the way to the gate.

Making herself run up the path, she opened the door, shouting, 'Happy birthday! Happy birthday!'

But there was no reply. The cottage was silent.

'Grandmother! Blodwen!' she called, going from room to room.

The log fire blazing in the big fireplace failed to register. All that got through was the feeling of being alone. In panic, she turned to go.

'She must have missed the train.' It was her grandmother's voice, and Claire guessed that they had been to the station to meet her.

'I came on the bus,' she said, greeting them at the door.

'We didn't want you to arrive on your own, child.' Her grandmother's arms held for her for a moment. 'Let me look at you.' She clucked her tongue. 'You're far too thin.'

'Happy birthday, Grandmother,' Claire said, dropping the small package into her grandmother's hand and kissing her again.

'How exciting!' Mrs Grant began to remove

the tissue wrappings with the same delight as a small child opening a Christmas stocking. 'Blodwen gave me this beautiful cardigan. Knitted it herself.'

'It's lovely, darling,' Claire said, the brittle note back in her voice as she watched the little leather box being unwrapped.

Pressing the metal catch, Mrs Grant opened the lid. Inside, against the dark velvet lining lay a brooch in silver and enamel, a replica of the wings worn on Martin's tunic.

'I know he would have liked you to have it,' Claire said, making an effort to sound casual, to keep things on a low key.

'And I'll be proud to wear it. So very proud,' her grandmother said, her voice not entirely steady.

The difficult moment was over, but Claire felt uneasy in the house.

'Do you mind if I go down to the sea for a few minutes before lunch?' she said.

'Is it a good idea?' her grandmother asked anxiously. 'There's a very cold wind.'

'There won't be a repeat performance, I promise you.'

Her grandmother turned her head away, but not before Claire had caught the pained expression.

'Sorry, darling,' she said. 'You mustn't

take any notice of me. I just need a few minutes on my own.'

Her grandmother nodded her understanding.

'Lunch in half an hour,' Blodwen called. 'Prompt, mind.'

'Time enough,' Claire said.

She walked briskly at first, but on the top of the bridge she paused. It seemed such a short time since that first leave at the cottage. Slowly she descended the wooden steps, her hand on Martin's letter still unopened in her pocket.

Climbing the concrete steps of the sea wall she walked to the far end where she and Martin had swum in the tossing waves. She sat on the bank of pebbles and took the letter from her pocket. To open it, to read this final letter, would be the last Goodbye. She sat a while, fingering the envelope, her hands trembling.

A sudden gust of wind tore the flimsy paper from her grasp, launching it in crazy flight. Desperately, Claire made a frantic grab, scrambling over the shifting pebbles. She wanted that letter more than anything else in the world. It was her own fault; now she would lose it without ever reading the contents.

But the envelope lodged between two stones. With a strangled cry she fell on it sobbing with relief. Her numb fingers fumbled with the flap, pulling out the single sheet of paper. She could hear his voice deep inside her head as she began to read:

Darling Claire,

It feels strange to be writing a letter which I hope you may never read, but I don't want to go without saying Goodbye.

I want the White Cottage to be yours — a home maybe, or a place to bring your children in the holidays. I know Father will never settle in the country, and it is with his full approval that I make this arrangement.

Be happy Claire. Don't grieve — but remember me sometimes. Most of all, remember the good times.

All my love,
Martin

A short letter, and — like the card with the red roses — very much to the point. And yet, it was all there — all she wanted to hear. Yes. To hear. He was speaking to her as clearly as though he was beside her. Remember the good times: long summer days, and picnics in the sandhills; growing up together — happy without ever thinking about happiness — taking it for granted;

their first kiss; the cottage . . . yes . . . the cottage.

Carefully, she replaced the letter in its envelope and put it back into her pocket. Even the hissing of the spent waves sucking back the shingle touched the past.

She climbed the wall and walked back, remembering.

'Did you enjoy your walk?' Mrs Grant enquired. She had been watching from the window as Claire came up the path.

Pausing at the door, Claire stared at her grandmother, knowing in that moment that the visit to the cottage in the depths of winter had been no mere whim, but deliberate strategy.

'You . . . you arranged this for my benefit.'

'Nonsense!'

But they both knew it was not nonsense. The bond between them had never been stronger.

'Will you take care of this for me?' Claire said, taking the sapphire ring from her finger.

Her grandmother nodded and took the ring without comment.

When Claire returned to Preslan that evening she had not lost the emptiness which Martin's death had left, but life was no longer all in shades of grey. One chapter of her life had closed. Her acceptance of this allowed the past to regain some sort of perspective; the happy glimpses of earlier days were no longer totally rejected. A new Claire was emerging, but the protective shell remained.

Colonel Turner had written regularly. In each letter he mentioned the cottage, with increasing hope that Claire might change her mind. There was a letter from him the day after her grandmother's birthday. He had been expecting a posting to the United States, and now it had come. On embarkation leave, he hoped to hand over the cottage before his departure.

Respecting Martin's last wish, Claire agreed. So, it was finally settled and in the next few weeks Claire went several times to visit the little house. Sometimes Ivor would be there working in the garden, and sometimes she would be on her own. She shared the Colonel's opinion that it was wrong to leave the house empty for the greater part of the year, and it was with this in mind that she approached her grandmother when she went home on a thirty-six hour pass.

'I just don't know what to do about the cottage,' she said, adding, half seriously, 'I suppose you and Blodwen wouldn't like to go there to live?'

'Permanently?' her grandmother said, frowning. 'That would hardly be fair to you.'

'To me?' Claire said. 'But, darling, it would be the perfect answer from my point of view. No. It was a crazy idea. Forget I even mentioned it. It just wouldn't be right to uproot you.'

'This house is getting too much for us,' her grandmother said. 'Too much — both physically and financially. It has been worrying me a great deal. My income has dwindled since the war began. There will be very little left for you and Blodwen when I am gone.'

Claire was stunned. 'Why didn't you tell me before?'

She had always considered her grandmother to be comfortably off: not wealthy, but having sufficient for her needs and with a little over. But as they discussed the position it became obvious that there had been no exaggeration. Her grandmother was almost penniless.

'And you kept all this to yourself?'

Claire could not imagine how this situation could have developed without even a hint of what was going on.

'It was my problem,' her grandmother said.

'There's the money Daddy left in his Will. I'll be twenty-one this year, and then it's mine to use as I wish. I'd like you to have it.'

'My dear child, I wouldn't touch a penny of it. There's little enough. Your father never could manage money. If only he'd bought the house when he had the opportunity.'

'Well, if you won't take the money, moving to the cottage would be doing me a great favour.'

'You're quite sure that is what you want?'

'There's not a doubt in my mind, and if you sold this house, the proceeds would give you some extra income. You could move whenever it suits you. Let's see what Blodwen has to say about it.'

Blodwen was all for moving at once; the next day would hardly have been soon enough for her. However, there was much to be done. That evening they went through the house, room by room, listing what was quite unsuitable for the cottage, the things they would be glad to be rid of, and the possessions which would go with them to Wales.

Once the decision was made there seemed no point in delay. The house was put on the market. Being well built and relatively undamaged by the raids, it quickly sold.

Claire came home on her days off and, with the three of them sorting, packing and discarding, the clearing was soon completed. One small van collected the things they were keeping, and arrangements were made for the remainder to be taken to the Sale Rooms.

'It's been a long time,' Mrs Grant said, finally closing the front door and turning away.

Claire was anxious until she saw her grandmother sitting in the rocking chair at the cottage.

'So good to feel at home again,' Mrs Grant said contentedly, rocking herself gently beside the log fire.

Claire knew that her grandmother and Blodwen were amongst friends. There was none of the isolation of town life. As for herself, she needed a fresh start, new faces — but no more close relationships. She was going to offer no hostage to fortune. The time had come to apply for a posting.

'Why not apply for that course in Dorset?' Janet said when Claire told her that she was hoping to make a move. 'I've put my name down.'

'Any idea what it is?' Claire asked.

'Not a clue.'

Claire laughed. 'Serve us right if it turns out to be concentrated spud-bashing.' But she added her name to the list.

The spring of 1944 found Claire saying Goodbye to friends who had helped her through the darkest days. As the truck turned out of the drive she and Janet waved to Dusty who was standing on the verandah. They were sad to be leaving the small friendly community, but curious to know what lay ahead on this mysterious course.

9

Wartime travelling was unpredictable and never more so than in the spring of 1944 when rumours of a second front were reinforced by the concentration of troops in the southern counties. The trains were packed with service men and women on the move.

Missing their scheduled train by two minutes, Claire and Janet found that there were long delays for connections. It was early evening before they reached the Dorset coast.

Judging from the clusters of kitbags on the station platform it seemed that they were not the only volunteers. They were all directed to an office close to the station and from there to various requisitioned houses in the town.

Claire and Janet were sent to the same house. Pointed in the general direction, they were left to find their own way. Cold and tired, they had to carry their kitbags, ground sheets, steel helmets and respirators through the streets, hunting for the house which was to be their base for the duration of the course.

'I can't walk another yard,' Claire said, dumping everything onto the pavement.

'Say! Going my way?' A GI driving a jeep drew up alongside, the well-applied brakes indicating an expertise that came of much practice.

Janet showed him the slip of paper with their new address.

'We'd be very grateful if you could drop us in that direction,' she said.

'Yes, Ma'am! Right to the door,' he said, jumping down and hauling their kit aboard. 'Let's go!'

The jeep took the hill like a mountain goat, and with the same abandon.

'Lew Mason,' the GI said by way of introduction as they slewed around a corner with a scattering of loose gravel.

'Janet Preston and Claire Grant,' Claire yelled, clutching the side of the vehicle.

They were thrown forward as the brakes slammed on and the jeep drew up outside a large stone-built house surrounded by a high wall.

'This is it,' Lew said, unloading the luggage. 'Gee! They let you carry all this?'

Claire grinned and nodded. 'They insist,' she said. 'Thank you for the lift.'

'You're welcome,' he said, touching his cap in a theatrical salute. 'See you around.'

The house looked little short of derelict, its garden overgrown and bedraggled. Inside the front hall their footsteps on the tiles echoed back from the bare walls.

'Not exactly home from home,' Janet said.

Claire pulled a long face. 'To think we left Preslan for this!'

A door at the top of the house slammed. Footsteps trailed along the landing and down a flight of stairs, the sound magnified by the bare boards. Curtains were being closed, increasing the gloom, until a solitary blue-tinted light was switched on, showing a Waaf coming down into the hall.

'Are you just posted in?' she enquired.

Janet looked down at the assorted luggage and back to the Waaf on the stairs.

'OK!' the girl said. 'I know. Ask a silly question . . . ' She pointed up the stairs. 'There's an empty room with two beds on the first landing. It's next to the bathroom I'm afraid. A bit noisy.'

'I could sleep with a trombone playing in my ear right now,' Claire said, dragging her kitbag behind her and hauling herself up the stairs with Janet close at her heels.

It was too late for supper by the time they had settled in. They still had the remnants of the packed meal prepared in the kitchen at the Preslan hostel, and that was enough to see them through to the morning.

Breakfast was in a large requisitioned house at the other end of the town, and then followed a morning of the usual routine when posted to a new station: getting chits signed, trailing from one office to another.

After lunch Claire and Janet joined a group of other new arrivals to be transported in trucks to the technical site outside the town.

On that journey each one of them was filled with misgivings. 'Never volunteer' had so often been good advice. As new recruits, too many of them had been caught by the request: 'Anyone here drive a car?' — only to find themselves spud-bashing, peeling mountains of potatoes in the coldest corner of a vast cookhouse; or, armed with mop and bucket, sent to clean the ablutions.

They knew nothing about the course; only the vaguest rumours had filtered through, and they had long since learned to mistrust rumour. When the truck came to an abrupt halt in a farmyard with poultry scattering in every direction, even the most optimistic began to wonder.

'This *can't* be it,' Janet said incredulously as the tailboard of the truck was unhitched.

But she was wrong. They were led beyond

the farmhouse to the largest of the group of huts scattered over the hilltop, where they were subjected to a tough lecture on security before being in any way enlightened. Later in the afternoon they were told what their future work would entail, and were introduced to the new radar equipment.

'Oboe . . . blind bombing!' Janet said. 'Working with Pathfinders. I never imagined anything like that, did you?'

Claire shook her head, viewing it all with oddly mixed feelings.

She sat at the console fingering the controls, imagining what was to come. 'Attack instead of defence,' she said, speaking her thoughts aloud, still unable to grasp completely the significance of this about-face. She wanted to see the war over and won, however hollow the victory might seem to her; but it was more than that. Was there a tinge of revenge in her excitement? The war had robbed her of so much. Now, at last, she was going to get a chance to reply. However, the feeling of satisfaction was not entirely untrammelled by guilt. It brought back vivid memories of the Merseyside blitz, and she pictured a young German girl in the same tangle of terror. It was not a comforting thought.

'Hey! Are you dreaming?' Janet asked,

shaking Claire's shoulder. 'Get a move on! The others have gone down to the truck.'

The course took all their concentration, not only operating the equipment, but becoming familiar with a slide rule until each operator could unravel complicated formulae at speed, converting a string of figures to give the information they required. Wind speed, height, curviture of the earth; things they had never before considered became second nature to them.

The whole area was seething with troops. Tension was growing and there was much talk of the second front. The atmosphere was charged with emotion; anxiety and excitement vied for supremecy. Eat, drink and be merry, for tomorrow . . . who knows?

'Come to the dance at the hotel on the headland?' Janet said to Claire one evening. 'That Canadian I met the other day, he's going.' She paused, continuing in an off-hand way: 'And he's got this friend, just arrived . . . '

'Are you suggesting a blind date?' Claire said.

'Well . . . yes. Come on. Let's have some fun. All work and no play . . . ' She peered into the mirror, combing her hair into a smooth roll around her head. 'You hardly ever go out these days.'

Reluctantly, Claire agreed to go, and the two Canadians arrived promptly at eight. The 'blind date' was not Claire's type, nor was she his, but having a good time was the order of the day. They laughed a lot, drank rather too much, and danced cheek to cheek on the crowded floor. They were more like puppets than real people: puppets on a stage, manipulated by some unseen hand.

'Better than mooning about in the billet, wasn't it?' Janet said the following day when they were discussing the friendly atmosphere of the hotel. 'They want us to go again on Saturday.'

'Leave me out of it,' Claire said. 'I don't want to get involved.'

'A couple of evenings' dancing. You can't call that 'getting involved'.'

'I mean it.'

'You'd think I was suggesting a mad bacchanalian night out.'

'Hardly that.'

'Then come on Saturday. There'll be a crowd of us there. Safety in numbers.'

Claire threw up her hands. 'Anything for a quiet life,' she said. 'What does it matter, anyway?'

And so the pattern was set. Work hard, play hard. But all the time Claire was reinforcing a wall around herself: on the surface, a load of fun; underneath, the Snow Queen. She tried to convince the world that the past was buried, that she was enjoying life, and to bolster her morale she drank too much and too often.

Late one Saturday evening she was with the usual crowd at the hotel when a GI came across and put a hand on her shoulder.

'Say! How are you getting along?' he said.

It was Lew Mason, the American who had given them a lift when they first arrived.

'Just fine and dandy, Lew my boy,' she said, trying to copy his Southern drawl.

'Will you shake a leg with me?' he asked, offering her his arm.

'I sho' will.'

She knew she was making a fool of herself and she didn't care.

'Can you jitter-bug?' Lew asked.

She nodded. 'But they won't allow it here.'

He winked. 'I didn't hear you,' he said, spinning her around and backing off, shaking his shoulders, still holding onto her hand.

The small orchestra played along, hotting up the pace. The other dancers moved back, giving them more room to manoeuvre. Claire whirled out and back. Lew took her by the waist, swinging her to his shoulder, her feet high in the air. The beat of the drums got louder and louder until, with one prolonged flourish and a crash of cymbals, it was all over.

Breathless, Claire clung to Lew and, laughing, they returned to the table at the edge of the floor where the management waited to forbid any repeat performance. However, it had been quite a hit with the patrons and only the strains of a dreamy waltz put an end to their cries for 'More! More!'

A group of US Army Air Force officers stood at the bar watching. One of them detached himself from his friends and walked across to speak to Claire.

'That was quite something,' he said. 'What are you drinking?'

Claire, ignoring the pass, looked around for Lew, but he was on the floor with Janet, demonstrating that he could dance a quiet waltz with the best of them. She smiled at the sight and, turning back, found that her glass had been replenished, and the tall American was sitting beside her.

'You don't waste any time, do you?' she said coolly.

'Here today, gone tomorrow.' He shrugged his shoulders, amused by her sudden change of manner, confident that he could reverse the trend once more.

His words were spoken lightly, but they struck a weak patch in her defences. She drained the glass and, to hide her feelings, asked: 'Well, aren't you going to ask me to dance?'

'But, of course.'

Rising a little unsteadily to her feet, Claire realized too late that she had had far too much to drink. The music drifted into a slow foxtrot; her partner steered her expertly around the floor, holding her much too close for her peace of mind. A befuddled panic set in. The sweet nothings he murmured in her ear indicated in which direction his mind was progressing.

'I must get back to my friends,' she said as the refrain dwindled away.

Ignoring her protests he led her to the bar. Her head was swimming and she pushed away the glass he tried to put in her hand.

'I must go,' she said, looking around wildly for some familiar face. Her voice sounded shrill in her ears.

'I'll get the keys of the jeep.'

'No, you won't.' The red-haired officer who had been watching Claire's performance on the dance floor insinuated himself between the two of them.

He waved away the opposition. 'So, she

asked for it,' he said to the frustrated Romeo, 'but she's not your type, and she's had more liquor than she can hold.'

He took Claire by the arm. 'You're coming with me,' he said, and turning to the barman, added: 'Black coffee in the lounge. OK?' and before Claire could protest she was shepherded away from the noise to the adjoining room.

'Just what are you trying to prove?' he asked, with a mixture of curiosity and impatience.

'And who asked you to interfere?'

'Somebody needs to tell you a thing or two,' he said. 'You ought to be at home with your mother.'

Claire winced. She wanted to hit out at him. She felt confused and angry. 'You Americans!' she said. 'You know it all, don't you?'

'Well, *you* don't,' he said. 'There's nothing surer than that.'

'It took Pearl Harbour to wake you up, and now . . . '

'Let's leave Pearl Harbour out of this,' he cut in.

'You think you've got the answers to everything.'

'So we've been told . . . frequently,' he said with a weary smile. 'Thank God our women aren't like you. Hard as . . . '

'Hard!' she interrupted, pausing as the waiter put down the tray of coffee, and waiting until he was out of earshot before continuing: 'Yes, I suppose I am hard. Maybe I was a different person before the war. But that was before my parents and little brother were torn apart by the bombs; before my fiancé was killed in a stupid road accident in the blackout.'

She stopped abruptly, realizing that she was being maudlin. The outburst sobered her.

'I'm talking too much,' she said, ashamed at the way the alcohol had loosened her tongue. 'I think you'd better pour that coffee.'

He lifted the coffee pot. 'I'm sorry,' he said, filling the two cups on the tray. 'I guess I was too quick with the criticism.'

'Forget the sympathy,' she said. 'I can stand anything but that.'

'Mud in your eye!' he said, raising the small cup and draining the contents. He choked. 'They call this coffee?' he gasped, putting down the cup and lifting the lid of the pot to look inside.

It relieved the tension. Claire laughed weakly.

'Think yourself lucky,' she said. 'We don't

often get such a treat.'

'In that case, I'm glad your need is greater than mine. Are you ready for some more punishment?'

Claire handed her cup over for a refill. 'I don't even know your name,' she said.

'David Powell.'

'But that's a Welsh name, surely?'

'Blame my Welsh grandfather for that.'

'I'm Claire Grant. My home is in Wales,' she said, and found herself telling him about the cottage.

It was some time later when she looked at her watch, and gasped, 'Heavens! Is that the time? I haven't got a late pass. I've had it if I'm found out at this time.'

'Don't worry. I'll take you back.'

The fresh air struck Claire like a sledge hammer.

'Say! You really did hit the bottle,' David said, putting his arm around her to steady her.

'Don't start that again,' she snapped. 'I've had enough of your lecturing for one night.'

'Steady!' he said. 'I thought we were getting on OK.'

Claire concentrated on her balance, but the lack of light was no help. David looked for the jeep, but someone else must have had a set of keys. It had already gone. However, the billet was no great distance away, and Claire needed the walk to clear her head.

'Can I see you again?' David asked when they got to the gate.

Claire paused with her hand on the latch. He had made no attempt to kiss her, and for this she was grateful. At least he'd had no ulterior motive in helping her.

'I don't think it would be a good idea,' she said, and there was a finality about her reply which turned him away with a shrug and a casual wave, but without another word.

'Where have you been?' Janet asked, sitting up in bed as Claire stumbled into the room.

'Around,' Claire said flatly.

'I don't know which way to take that. You're a dark horse.'

'Don't go on about it, please . . . ' Claire's voice broke.

'You didn't go off with that wolf in American Air Force clothing, did you?'

'Not the one you mean.'

'I did rather lose track!'

Claire picked up her towel. 'I'm going for a bath,' she said irritably.

'You can't — unless you'd like it stone-cold. There's no hot water.'

'Damn!' Claire sat on her bed and began to cry, quietly.

'Are you all right?' Janet asked. Getting no reply, she sat up. 'Get into bed, Claire. You've had too much to drink. That's all that's wrong with you.'

'Don't you start too.'

'It was the one with the red hair, wasn't it?' Janet sighed. 'The one with the come-to-bed eyes. He looked as though he was talking to you like a Dutch uncle.'

Claire said nothing. She didn't want to think about those steady grey eyes.

'You going out with him again?' Janet yawned and snuggled down under the bedclothes once more.

'What do you mean — again?' Claire said. 'And the answer is no.'

'Pity. He seemed rather nice. Goodnight. Sleep well.'

But it was a long time before Claire got off to sleep. Her head swam, and she swore never again to drink so much, to allow things to get so out of control.

10

On their next day off Janet decided to take the train to Bournemouth to do some shopping, but Claire wanted time on her own, a day to walk and allow the fresh air to blow away the cobwebs in her mind.

Spring had arrived. The air was soft and warm. She walked along the cliff path, shedding her jacket and cap, rolling up her shirt sleeves and feeling the sun caress her skin. Stopping at her favourite spot, further from the town than most people ventured, she sat on the smooth block of stone she knew so well and, completely relaxed, looked out over the sea. The approaching footsteps were almost alongside before she looked up. It was David Powell, smiling down at her.

'Your friend Janet said you liked this walk. I've been up here every day hoping to see you.'

'I'll have words with Janet,' Claire said, and frowned. 'How did you come to meet her?'

'That was the easy part.'

'Don't you Americans ever take no for an answer?'

He grinned, sitting on the stone beside her. 'You British don't have the monopoly on obstinacy. We can be every bit as stubborn as you.'

'You've been up here every day?'

He nodded.

'You don't do much work then?'

'Even we are allowed some time off. Three more days and I go back to my unit in Norfolk.'

'On leave! And you've been wasting time hanging around waiting for me?' Claire was embarrassed.

'Not wasting time. After all, here's today almost untouched. Couldn't we give ourselves just one day?'

'If I agree, I don't want you to get the wrong idea.'

'No strings,' he said.

'No strings.' She laughed, and was suddenly serious again. 'I mean what I say, David.'

'You're a strange kid. O.K. by me. It's your day. What d'you want to do with it?'

'I'd like to walk,' she said. 'But, it's your leave. You choose.'

'A walk suits me.'

'Over the hills?'

He nodded. 'With lunch at one of your English country pubs.'

A lark was singing high above their heads, reminding Claire of the White Cottage, and of Martin, seldom far from her thoughts.

'Come back,' David said, squeezing her arm gently.

She looked up at him half apologetically and, as quickly, looked away. 'Just remembering,' she said.

For a while they walked on in silence — a companionable silence with no need for words. It was only broken when, reaching a high point, they looked down on a cluster of stone-built cottages.

'I knew there had to be a scene like that somewhere in the world,' David said, holding his hands up to frame the view.

The dip of the hills at either side gave a distant glimpse of the sea, sparkling in the sunshine. From their vantage point they could see the narrow road meandering down, over the bridge which crossed the sparkling stream and through the hamlet to the inn, with the parish church set back amongst the trees.

'I hope they haven't run out of beer,' David said.

'An American who actually likes British beer! I don't believe it.'

'You can get used to anything if you put your mind to it.'

139

'A remark like that could get you lynched in a place like this.'

They paused at the old stone bridge to look down into the clear water bubbling over the stones, then continued up the gentle slope towards the inn. The narrow street was deserted.

'Mornin', sir,' the landlord said as David investigated the bar. 'And what can I get you?'

'We were hoping for some lunch.'

The man rubbed his chin. 'There now! We don't get much passing trade in the middle of the day. Not in these times.' He gave a reassuring nod. 'Hold on a minute. I'll see how they're fixed in the kitchen.'

Moments later he returned, smiling broadly. 'You're in luck. We've got a nice piece of beef, and the wife's rhubarb pie to follow. How would that be?'

David looked at Claire.

'Perfect,' she said.

The landlord put his head around the door and shouted the order through to the kitchen.

Claire sat on a wooden bench beside the window.

'What can I get you to drink?' David said.

'Shandy, I think. Yes, a nice cool lemonade shandy.'

They sat quenching their thirst in the bar, and it was not long before the dining room door was opened by a girl in a crisp, flower-printed apron.

'It's all ready, sir,' she said, showing them to their table.

It was a simple meal with vegetables fresh from the garden. Finishing the first course, David began his helping of pie.

'The only thing missing is the cream,' he said, cutting through the crisp pastry with his fork and wincing a little at the sharpness of the fruit. 'And a little more sugar,' he added.

The rhubarb was young and red: thin sticks with plenty of flavour, but certainly not very sweet.

'You're spoilt! Haven't you heard of sugar rationing?' Claire said with a chuckle.

When they had finished their meal they set off once more, past the church and the stone wall surrounding the manor house. The classic lines of the house were obscured by the trees, but every now and again there was a teasing glimpse of the sunlit facade.

'That could only be England,' David said, getting a full view of the house at the end of an avenue of trees. 'England in the spring. I've heard about it so often. The time to see Vermont is in the fall. You should see it . . . colours you never knew existed.'

'Have you been to Wales yet?'

David shook his head. 'But I plan to go on my next furlough.'

'Do you know anyone there? Have you any relatives still living in Wales?'

'None that I know of, but my father would never forgive me if I went back home without visiting the places his pa used to tell him about.'

'I'll give you my grandmother's address,' Claire said. 'I'm sure she'd be delighted to see you.' She stopped abruptly, aware that, despite her original intent, already she was becoming involved.

David seemed to sense her disquiet and turned the conversation in another direction. 'Time we were heading back,' he said. 'We've got quite a distance to cover. I hope you won't be too tired to come out to dinner with me tonight?'

'Not so fast!' Claire said in alarm. 'David . . . I'm not sure that I could face the hotel after my exhibition the other evening.'

The memory obviously amused him. He smiled, his eyes teasing her until she had to laugh herself.

'I don't know what got into me,' she said. 'Although, come to think of it, I suppose I'd been working up to it for some time.'

He put an arm around her waist, striding a little slower.

'I've got the jeep for the evening,' he said. 'I guessed you might prefer to go somewhere new.'

'You were so sure of your charms.' There was a touch of acid in her voice.

'Now, don't get me wrong!' he protested. 'I wasn't sure of anything. It's not the first day I've tried to see you. Remember?'

'Yes, I remember. Wasting all that time. You crazy man.'

'Well, thanks! That's what I like. Honest appreciation.' He looked down at her, laughing.

Claire laughed too. They stood in the middle of the deserted road and as their laughter died away it took with it some of Claire's defences.

'No.' It was a word spoken to herself. She pushed his arm from her waist and walked on. 'David, perhaps it would be better if we didn't see each other again,' she said, looking straight ahead.

'What have I done? For crying out loud! What have I said?' His normally relaxed features were strained. 'If I've offended you, then I'm sorry . . .'

'It's nothing like that. I just don't want to get involved.'

'That goes for me too. Buddies . . . that's all.' His voice was casual now.

She couldn't look at him. In her head, she was hearing a snatch of the song: ' . . . let's be buddies . . . and leave it to fate how it ends . . . '

'The main road must be up ahead,' David said. 'Just listen to that.' The steady rumble of a convoy of heavy trucks reached them before they sighted the road. 'The second front can't be far away now. Soon the war in Europe will be over, and then . . . '

'And then, we'll all go home,' Claire said, and wondered why the thought appalled her. Peace. It had seemed so remote; she had never really given much thought to life in post-war Britain. She had pictured no life beyond the war. Now, she was always surrounded by friends, excitement, always something new. All right, war was a good fifty per cent boredom, but at least the discipline left little time for brooding. Peace. That was something altogether different. The thought frightened her.

Reaching the busy road, they waited for a bus to take them back into the town. When it arrived it was full to the door and swept past without so much as slowing down.

'Well, you did say you wanted a walk,' David said. But he had hardly closed his

144

mouth when a jeep pulled up beside them.

'Hey, Bud! Want a lift?' the GI said, and moments later they were overtaking the bus and everything else on the road. The driver's foot remained hard on the accelerator until they reached the town centre. 'This OK?' he asked.

'Fine,' David said. 'Thanks.'

Claire marvelled at the lack of formality and imagined the rocket an unfortunate British soldier would get if he addressed an officer in that same casual way. She had even had to be careful when she went out with Martin, as officers and the ranks were not officially permitted to mix socially.

'I don't think I could have managed it on my two feet,' she said, smiling at the GI. 'Thank you for the lift.'

'You're welcome, ma'am.' The man touched his cap in what was part wave, part salute. 'Well! What d'you know?' he said, looking beyond them to the reason for his hurry. A tall blonde, with curves in all the right places, was waving to him.

David took Claire's arm in his and walked with her back to the billet.

'I'll call for you at seven-thirty. O.K.?'

'I'll be ready,' she said.

As she had expected, the furnace was out. She had hoped for a warm bath, but it had been a slender hope, instead she had to content herself with a chilly splash in five inches of cold water. However, it had the virtue of making her tingle all over, and she returned to her room refreshed.

Janet was still out and had not returned by the time Claire was ready and could see David standing down by the gate.

'I haven't kept you waiting, have I?' she asked, running down the path.

'Only five minutes late. Not bad,' he said, studying her with an appreciative eye. 'Not bad at all.' He whistled under his breath.

As far as the weather went, the day was not living up to its earlier promise. On the horizon where the sea and sky met, there was a dark line.

'Dirty weather on the way,' David said. 'Are you going to be warm enough?'

'We're not going far, are we?'

'I booked a table at an inn about six or seven miles away I guess.'

'Then, I'll be all right.'

The sky got darker. The jeep took to the hills, and the storm broke as they pulled into the yard of the inn.

'Come on,' David said, lifting Claire down from the jeep. 'It can only get worse at this stage. Let's make a dash for it.'

The blackout curtains were already drawn.

Despite the weather, the bar was full, and in the adjoining dining room theirs was the only vacant table. The electric lights flickered and there was a crash of thunder.

'Light up the candles, Nora,' the landlord called out, turning to his customers and adding, 'Every time we have a storm the electricity seems to fail.'

As he spoke the lights went off, and a cheer broke out as the lighted candles appeared.

'Let's go through to our table,' David said, helping Claire to get across the crowded room. 'And I thought this was going to be a quiet evening! It gets more like Grand Central Station every minute.'

They sat down.

The waitress closed the door leading from the bar, and the noise level dropped at once.

Claire looked up to find David studying her across the candlelit table. His gaze was so intense that she turned her head away, confused, angry with herself for being caught off balance.

'Are you ready to order, sir?' the waitress asked.

Claire was glad of the few moments it took to order the meal, making David concentrate his attention elsewhere. After that, she took care to keep the conversation on general

147

lines. She told David more about her grandmother and Blodwen, and of their recent move to the White Cottage. And when he asked about Martin she found herself filling in the details as though they belonged to a different existence, unconnected with the present. He, in turn, told her of his family and home in Vermont: the white colonial style house set in a background of hills, with his studio down by the river where he painted in his spare time; his job with an advertising agency in New York.

The evening went quickly. The candle was guttering in the squat candlestick, the power not yet restored, when they heard the landlord calling, 'Time, gentlemen, please.'

'And time we were going,' Claire said briskly. 'I don't want to oversleep in the morning. It must be the air down here — makes me sleep like a baby.'

The storm had cleared, but the sky was overcast and it was very dark.

'I've got a torch somewhere,' she said, putting her hand into one of the pockets in her jacket, feeling for the small torch she always carried at night. The feeble light, dimmed by a double layer of tissue stretched beneath the glass to comply with regulations, was almost useless.

'Put that away,' David said. 'I can see perfectly well.'

He put an arm around her, guiding her through the yard to the parked jeep.

'Are you free tomorrow evening?' he asked as he drove slowly out onto the road and accelerated towards the town.

'No, not tomorrow. I'm on duty.'

'Friday is my last day down here. Can you make that?'

'Yes, I think so.'

'I'll pick you up at seven-thirty.'

She felt safe in accepting. After all, they were unlikely ever to meet again.

'I'll be ready,' she said.

The jeep drew up near the billet. Claire felt herself stiffen as David's arm encircled her.

'Relax, Claire. We had a great time, didn't we?'

'Yes.'

'Then don't freeze on me. I haven't forgotten . . . no strings.'

'You think I'm cold? Crazy, maybe?'

'No. I think you've been mauled by this war.'

She leaned her head back against his shoulder. 'I wish I didn't like you quite so much.'

'Well, that's the craziest thing I've ever heard . . . but it kinda makes me hope.' His lips touched her cheek.

'See you on Friday,' she said, her voice barely above a whisper.

He turned her face to his and kissed her then, just once, a tender kiss made more electric by the clear restraint which held them both. And then she slipped from his grasp and ran into the billet. She stood inside the door, no Snow Queen now, the barrier against the world was under siege.

She told herself that they must not meet again, but on Friday evening she was ready early. She kept peering out of the window, but there was no sign of David. At last, she went down into the hall to get a better view along the path.

'You haven't seen an American waiting outside, have you?' she asked one of the girls who had just come in.

The airwoman shook her head, and then she paused. 'Oh! You're Corporal Grant, aren't you?' she said, frowning, as though trying to remember something. 'Yes. I remember. There was a letter for you this morning. I think it was left on the table down here.'

'It's not here now,' Claire said.

The girl shrugged. 'There was an inspection this morning — a bit of a flap. I expect it got tidied away.'

It was clear that David was not coming. Claire spent some time searching for the letter and enquiring in each room before giving up.

So. That was it. He must have been recalled from leave. Or, maybe he thought it had all gone far enough. She was sorry not to have said Goodbye, but perhaps it was better that way. No strings. No entanglements.

11

The course was over and postings were imminent.

Through the window, Claire could see Janet running up the path. Her footsteps echoed in the hall below, and moments later she burst into the room with the news.

'The postings are through,' she said, sitting on the end of her bed to get her breath back. 'You asked for the station near Dover, didn't you?'

'Yes.'

'I did too,' Janet said, pulling out the things from her locker and beginning to sort through her clothes.

'Are you going to tell me, or are you not?' Claire said impatiently.

'We're both going to Norfolk.'

The two girls looked at each other and fell about laughing.

'Might have known this would happen,' Claire said. 'When do we leave?'

Although Claire had applied for a posting to Kent, the thought of going to Norfolk was not unwelcome. Norfolk made her think of The Fens, of boating on The Broads, cold winds from the North Sea — those not so inviting; and, not least, she thought of David. Did she want to meet him again? Perhaps it was as well that a meeting seemed such a remote possibility. Neither knew where the other was stationed.

'We have to get cleared tomorrow, and we leave first thing on Thursday,' Janet said. 'A good job our laundry has just come back, but I'll have to wash this lot somehow and I'm almost out of soap.'

'Sorry. I haven't a spare soap coupon,' Claire said, 'but try this.' She handed a small bottle to Janet.

'Hair shampoo?'

'Try it. It's perfect for woollen things and stockings.'

'Why didn't I think of that before?' Janet said when she returned from the bathroom with her washing done. 'Much better than a small sliver of soap.'

Wednesday was spent trailing around the town getting signatures on their clearance chits, and packing their kit for an early start the following morning.

The journey to Norfolk was one of the worst they had encountered. Troop trains had priority. They arrived at Great Yarmouth on the last train of the day to find everything closed down and the telephone out of order.

153

The only other person to get off the train was a Squadron Leader who was waiting in the booking hall. When he saw Claire trying to use the telephone he walked across and enquired, 'Can I give you both a lift? My driver should be here any minute now. I'm on my way to Summerton. Any good to you?'

'That's our new posting,' Claire said. 'We were beginning to wonder if we'd ever make it.'

Summerton had been a holiday camp in peacetime: a string of bungalows behind the sandhills, some brick-built and others of wooden construction. But Claire and Janet could see none of this when they arrived at the Guard Room, where they signed in and waited for the duty NCO to arrive.

'Two corporals,' the voice behind them said with obvious displeasure, as though they were being purposely difficult. 'Wherever can I put you?'

'I really couldn't care less,' Janet said, as near to losing her temper as Claire had ever seen her. 'Just find *somewhere* before we drop.'

'Follow me.'

Hitching their respirators and steel helmets onto their shoulders and picking up the kitbags which felt as though they had

154

doubled in size since the morning, they followed the weak glow of the torch. The moon came out from behind a bank of cloud and it was possible to distinguish the outlines of the bungalows on one side, and the curved roofs of nissen huts on the other.

Stopping at last, they thought they had finished their long trail, but the halt was only to pick up clean sheets. The road ahead was again swallowed up in the darkness. A hundred yards further on Janet was left on the doorstep of a hut.

'There's a spare bed in the middle room,' the duty NCO said, shining her torch on a list she held in her hand. 'You should have a room of your own, but that will have to be sorted out later.'

Claire had another fifty yards to go. At the door she fumbled for her torch.

'It's the bed on the right as you go in,' the NCO whispered before vanishing into the night.

Everything was silent, and the whole place was in darkness.

Claire opened the door and crept inside. She was in a small lobby. Opening the inner door she was relieved to find the empty bed with its blankets neatly stacked at the head.

As quickly and quietly as she could, she made up the bed. The battery of her torch was almost spent, and she cursed herself for not buying a new one. Her pyjamas and washing things were packed at the top of her kit bag. No problem there. After brushing her teeth and a perfunctory wash at the cold tap in the lobby, she felt her way back, put off the fading torch and climbed between the sheets.

'Well! Where did you spring from?'

It was morning. Claire opened her eyes to see Edna, whom she had last seen at Danborough, standing at the end of her bed.

'Edna! How good to see you. How long have you been stationed here?'

'A couple of months. Are you coming to breakfast?'

'I'd give my back teeth for a bath.'

'Do you know the geography?'

'All I know is that this hut is a day's march from the Guard Room.'

'The bath huts are further down the road. The 'usual offices' are around the back, a lean-to on the end of the hut. Oh yes, and Dan comes this morning, so don't leave the windows open.'

'Dan?'

'Dan, Dan, the . . .'

'Message received and understood,' Claire said with a wry grin.

'There's a spare pair of gum boots in the lobby,' Edna said. 'You'd better have those, if they'll fit you. Put them on . . . and your greatcoat. I'll show you where the bath huts are. If you're quick, I'll wait to go to breakfast with you.'

Inside the first bath hut there were two long troughs with enamel basins at regular intervals; in addition, there were several cubicles, each containing a bath, a wooden duckboard, and a chair. The bare concrete floor struck cold, even through the heavy boots.

'I don't suppose the water will be very warm,' Edna said. 'You need to be here by six for a decent bath.'

There were no plugs for the baths, and Claire rummaged in her sponge bag for the recognized substitute: a penny folded in a handkerchief. The water had the chill off, but little more. She was not encouraged to linger, and fifteen minutes later she and Edna were making for the cookhouse.

'I'm not on duty until one o'clock,' Edna said. 'I'll show you where the Orderly Room is.'

'One to six?' Claire asked.

'Yes. Three watch at the moment.'

Claire pulled a face.

'It's not so bad on Oboe,' Edna said. 'At

157

least we know in advance when we're going to be busy. We're pretty well organized.'

They met Janet in the cookhouse. It took most of the morning to settle in, but by lunchtime they had not only dealt with all the form-filling but had also rearranged the sleeping accommodation so that all three had single rooms in the same hut.

In the afternoon they went up to the technical site to watch Pathfinder test runs on targets in Oxfordshire.

'Here! Work that out, Corporal,' the controller said, giving Claire a list of figures and a slide rule.

She produced the answer quickly.

'Good,' he said, checking with his own figures, and turning to the sergeant of the watch he asked, 'Any vacancies on this crew, Sergeant?'

'No, sir. We are up to strength, but Summerton Two and Three both need operators.'

'You'd better go to Summerton Two, Corporal.'

'Now, sir?'

'No time like the present. You know where it is?'

'Yes, sir. It was pointed out on our way up here.'

'Good. And . . . Corporal . . . don't try

any short cuts through the mine field. Two dogs got the chop last week.'

Claire got to Summerton Two only to find that she had forgotten about pass numbers, and she had to return to the Guard Room to get the number for the day. It was not a good start, but no one seemed unduly bothered.

It was too much to hope that Edna and Janet and she would end up on the same duty rota and so share the same day off, but from the look of the op's room it seemed unlikely that they would have much spare time in the foreseeable future. Pressure was building up, and soon the practice runs had to be fitted in between daylight raids and the night bombing.

After working on the practice runs, Claire was finally allowed to take part in the actual operation, guiding six Pathfinder Mosquitos to their target.

The first call sign went out and immediately a blip appeared on the cathode ray tube. 'Able Baker' was not far from the centre of the beam. Summerton was acting as the 'cat' or tracking station, keeping the Mosquito at a constant range, in an arc which would pass directly over the target. The dots of the signal gradually merged to a single note; then, as the aircraft flew through the beam the note changed to a series of dashes, indicating that the range must be decreased.

The sister Oboe station in Kent was the 'mouse' or release station, sending signals to the navigator to indicate the exact position on the beam and finally giving the signal for the release of the bombs or the target indicators, whichever were being carried.

Ten minutes to target, and the 'mouse' station transmitted four A's in morse code. The Mosquito was flying steadily along the beam. Four B's . . . eight minutes to go; four C's . . . six minutes. Tension increased with each signal; there was still time for something to go wrong: the rigidly plotted course made the Mosquito a predictable target. Four D's . . . only three minutes to go. 'Abel Baker' was dead on course. Then, five dots followed by a longer note which cut at the exact point of release.

'Cope!' the controller said with satisfaction, standing behind the operators and watching the screen. He studied the chronometer on the wall. 'Send out the next call-sign . . . *now*.'

In just over an hour, six aircraft were guided over the area. Five were successful — 'copes' — and one failed to switch on, whether because of a fault in the equipment or because of fighter activity it was impossible to know.

During that hour the concentration was intense, but there was no time to relax when it was all over; there was the next raid to set up, and another following that.

Claire wondered if she had ever felt so tired in all her life. Her head buzzed with the heavy hum of the transmitter. After the fourteen-hour night watch she went back to breakfast utterly exhausted. Returning to the hut she fell into bed and did not surface again until four in the afternoon.

'I thought you were going into Norwich today?' Janet said, putting her head around the door.

'I've had that!' Claire said, stretching her arms above her head. 'I never knew what it was like to be *really* tired before, but — Oh Boy! — I'm learning fast.'

'There's a truck coming up from one of the US air bases this evening,' Janet said. 'They've got a dance on. How about coming?'

'After my last effort!'

'Edna will be there.'

'Meaning that she'll keep an eye on me?'

'Given half a chance,' Janet said with a chuckle.

'I thought she was on duty tonight.'

'She's going into the Senior Controller's office from today . . . starts on the eight to one shift tomorrow, so she's got this evening off. Let's all go.'

After a little more persuasion, Claire agreed. She could not make up her mind whether she dreaded the chance of meeting David again, with the inevitable complications, or whether that was her reason for going. Whichever it was, the odds against meeting again were very high. This was only one of the many U.S. Army Air Force bases in the eastern counties.

If David was there, Claire did not see him.

'What's the matter, Claire?' Edna asked when they were climbing into the truck for the return journey. 'You look as though you've lost half a crown and found a ha'penny.'

'She hoped to meet her American heart-throb,' Janet said.

'And what happened to that air-crew type who used to write to you at Danborough?' Edna asked. 'You surely haven't chucked him?'

The moonlight caught the pain on Claire's face, the haunted look in her eyes.

'He was killed in a road accident,' Janet said, kicking herself for not realizing that Edna had known Claire when Martin was about.

'Oh, Claire!' Edna gasped. 'I'm so sorry.'

'Don't be,' Claire said. 'It helps to talk about Martin. People avoid mentioning him, but he's part of my life, and always will be.'

'You've grown up since Danborough.'

'Maybe.'

'And this American?'

'Just someone I met. I only knew him a short time. You know . . . ships that pass . . . '

'Sounds as though he made an impression.'

'He certainly did,' Janet said with conviction. 'But try to get her to admit it!'

The engine started up and further conversation was impossible. They clung to the truck sides for the uncomfortable journey back to camp.

All leave was now cancelled, mail was censored, and everyone knew that the second front — so long awaited — was about to open up. The massed bombers crossed the sky, some returning badly shot up, trailing smoke.

Claire often thought of David, wondering whether he might be up there carving a vapour trail high over the North Sea. The more she tried to put him out of her mind, the more he edged in. It was only when she was on duty that she completely forgot him. Life was hectic. There was barely time to complete one operation before the next one had to be set up.

When D Day came the burden of responsibility increased; with target indicators marking objectives in the battle zone there was no room for mistakes.

By the end of June everyone was feeling the strain but still they had to work at full stretch. It was a fight against time. Work and sleep.

'I want you on the tube for this one, Corporal,' the controller said as Claire arrived for duty for what looked like being a tough session.

The telephone rang.

'There's another batch through,' he said. 'Send someone over to the office for the bumf, and then we'll set this lot up.'

Summerton was the 'mouse' station this time, and it was Claire's job to press the button which gave the release signal. This was normally the controller's responsibility, but experiments were taking place to calculate whether the operator's view gave more accurate results.

Everything had been checked and counter-checked when the 'Cat' station sent out the call sign.

The Mosquito switched on. Claire watched the blip on the tube getting closer to the target. The most vital part of her job was to depress a switch at two precise moments; the release signal to the Mosquito was then automatically controlled.

A. B. C. D. The guiding signals went out at the correct intervals, and now the moment had almost come.

In her left hand Claire held a stop watch; in her right, cradled in the palm of her hand, the press-button switch. With a tight feeling in the pit of her stomach she watched for the moving blip to reach the exact position.

'Switch . . . one,' she said, pressing both thumbs instantaneously. Then, as the blip moved on to the next position: 'Switch . . . two.'

The release signal was transmitted.

'Cope,' the controller said. 'Good show.'

No time for relief. No time for congratulations. Someone else slid into Claire's chair, and the next call sign went out.

12

Although unrelenting, the raids were not spread evenly throughout the twenty-four hours. Inbetween times, the records had to be kept straight, the equipment serviced, the floors polished to make sure that there was no dust about, and the next batch of data had to be processed.

Days stretched into weeks. It was after those first tremendous pressures had settled into a steady pattern that Claire was asked to go to the Guard Room one morning. Still on a three watch system she had only got into bed at nine; being ordered to the Guard Room at eleven-thirty did not put her in the happiest of moods. Before she had a chance to ask what it was all about, the girl who had brought the message had gone.

Claire yawned and dragged herself out of bed. A quick bath. Her battle-dress needed pressing, so she decided to put on her best blue, not knowing quite what to expect.

Having walked the length of the camp she reported to the SP on duty outside the Guard Room.

'Someone to see you,' he said, opening the

door for her to go inside, and she could feel his resentment.

She found herself face to face with David, and something akin to an electric shock hit her with a force that took her breath away.

'You didn't write,' he said, 'so I had to find out where you were.'

'But . . . how?'

'Come out with me and I'll tell you.'

In a daze, Claire signed out of camp. David had a jeep parked near the main gate.

'I've discovered a little place called Potter Heigham,' he said. 'Do you like the water?'

She nodded. 'But, David, I want to know how you found me again.'

'I went to see your grandmother.'

'My grandmother? But I never got around to giving you her address.'

'The description you gave was enough. I got off the train at the right station, and the rest was child's play.' He flipped the ignition key in his hand. 'Your grandmother . . . she's quite a dame!'

Claire smiled. Her grandmother would relish that description.

'And how did you get on with Blodwen?'

He raised his eyebrows. 'I don't think Blodwen took to me at first, but when she heard my name and knew I was the grandson of a Welshman, that did it! I was home and dry.' He grinned at the memory.

'But, Claire,' he said, his face becoming serious, 'why didn't you write?'

'I heard that someone had left a note for me, and I guessed it must be from you, but I never got it. There was some stupid inspection and it must have got whisked away in a last-minute panic. I had no idea where you might be. Norfolk is a fairly large county.'

'If you had known, would you have written?'

'I . . . I don't know,' she said evasively, but then relented. 'I think . . . yes.'

'That's a start,' he said, slipping the jeep into gear. 'Let's go.'

At Potter Heigham David hired a small rowing boat. He rowed it out to a quiet stretch of water and shipped the oars.

The day was warm and only the lightest breeze tickled the surface of the Broads. The other boats were some distance away. There were only two people in the world at that moment. Claire knew that she was fighting a losing battle. She was caught in a web from which, to her surprise, she had no desire to escape. She sat very still looking into David's eyes, her hands gripping the sides of the boat. She tried to look away, to break the invisible bond which held them fast; she tried to make some banal remark to crush the life from the feelings that welled up inside her . . . but, it was no use. David was winning. She knew it. David knew it too.

'Don't . . . don't look at me like that,' she said at last.

He moved towards her and the boat rocked dangerously so that he had to sit down again.

'Goddam it! I want to kiss you,' he said, and grabbing the oars rowed for the jetty.

Tying up the boat, David climbed out and taking Claire's hands he pulled her ashore. Still holding her hands in his, he stood smiling down at her.

'No escape now,' he said, bending his head to kiss her full on the lips.

She made no attempt to discourage him. The rumble of aircraft in the distance reminded her that the war was not yet over. She was well aware that fate had an inexhaustible appetite for hostages. It would be sensible to break now, before the cycle of joy and sorrow spun out of control.

They lunched at the waterside pub. Later they walked past reed-thatched cottages, crossing the bridge to sit a while beneath the willow trees.

Claire lay back in the partial shade and closed her eyes.

'Hey! Lazybones,' David said, tickling the end of her nose with a piece of grass.

'I'll have you know I've had two hours sleep since the night before last,' Claire said indignantly.

'Did I get you out of bed?'

'You did,' she said, her eyes closing again.

'And nothing was further from my thoughts.' He kissed her eyelids, gently teasing.

'We said, no strings.' Slowly, she opened her eyes to his: grey, and serious now, gazing down at her with a mixture of tenderness and desire.

'We meant it . . . then,' he said.

The tender kiss deepened into a consuming, passionate embrace. The fire of the moment hit them both — an eruption of the senses, leaving them breathless.

For Claire there was a new dimension to living, something she had never felt before . . . even with Martin.

'You don't want me to apologize, do you?' David said, his eyes never leaving hers. There was a confidence about him which had nothing to do with arrogance. The slow smile told her that he needed no answer.

He frowned suddenly. 'I'm a selfish louse,'

he said. 'You must be exhausted. No sleep since the night before last. We've got all day. Close your eyes.' He kissed her, gently this time.

Through the branches of the overhanging tree the dappled sunlight was warm on her skin. A feeling of contentment embraced her. She drifted into sleep.

When she opened her eyes the sun was still high in the sky.

'It's not a dream?' she said, putting her hand out to touch David's face. 'Tell me it's not a dream.'

He took her in his arms and kissed the startled look from her face. 'Welcome to my dream . . . ,' he sang, laughing.

'You're not quite Bing Crosby,' she said, recognizing the song from 'The Road to Morocco', but you're not a bad substitute.'

'Like acorn coffee, or dried egg, I guess?'

'Oh, better. Much, much, better.'

'That's a comfort. And how would you feel about dinner in Norwich?'

'I haven't got a late pass.'

'O.K., Cinderella. I'll get you back in good time.'

In some ways he was so like Martin, she thought. And yet, there were depths which she could sense but which were, as yet, beyond her understanding: gentle kindness with an iron core, but so much more. There was something about him so unlike Martin's open, almost boyish nature. It would take time to know this man. Claire knew the time for retreat had gone . . . long gone.

They strolled back to the jeep and were in Norwich with time to spare for a walk through the cathedral close and to explore some of the narrow streets before dinner.

Their meal was interrupted by the banshee note of the air-raid siren, followed soon after by the uneven note of an engine which cut suddenly. A flying bomb crashed to earth some distance away. These pilotless aircraft packed with high explosive were programmed for selected targets, but the lack of any human control in chosing the precise position of cut-out made them both indiscriminate and spine-chilling.

David held Claire's hands across the table. The conversation around them was more hearty than before. Soon the 'all clear' sounded, and people relaxed again as though nothing had happened.

David looked at his watch. 'Time we were on the move,' he said. 'The pumpkin awaits, Cinderella.'

They were nearing Summerton when Claire asked: 'Do you think I'm a jinx, David?'

He pulled the jeep into the side of the

road. 'Don't ever say that,' he said angrily. 'Don't even think it.'

'I know it sounds crazy,' she said. 'But I can't help wondering. Ever since the beginning of the war . . . just one catastrophe after another. Keep away from me David. Keep away until it's all over.'

'Don't be a dope,' he said, taking her roughly by the shoulders. 'You're tired, but that's no excuse. You can talk yourself into any damn fool idea.'

'Sometimes I imagine what it must be like not to be afraid of saying Goodbye in case it's the last time.' She sighed. 'When this war is over . . . '

'When this war is over, you're coming back to Vermont with me.'

She wanted to believe him, but she knew that things would be very different when peace came.

'You'll marry some nice girl from your home town,' she said. 'Someone you've known all your life.'

He shook his head. 'I made up my mind the second time I saw you.'

'Just like that?'

'Just like that.' He started up the jeep.

It was some days later that Claire got a letter from her grandmother telling her of David's brief visit, which had clearly been a success; an invitation had been issued for him to stay on his next leave.

Claire needed time to adjust to the idea of David coming back into her life . . . perhaps for always. She had been completely knocked sideways by her feelings for him. After Martin's death, she had thought she could never love anyone else, but her love for David was altogether different — like nothing she had ever felt before. The fact that she had known him for such a short time seemed irrelevant. Those snatched moments together had no comparison with the rest of time.

It was this very unreal quality which Claire needed to eliminate. She needed to see David as he would be when there was no more war. Would he feel the same? Would she feel the same? She wanted to see him in the familiar surroundings of her own home. But, for Claire, leave was still impossible.

On duty the following day she was asked to take over from Edna in the Senior Controller's office. Puzzled by the order, she arrived at the office to find Edna ready to go.

'My mother's been injured by a flying bomb,' Edna said. 'I've got compassionate leave. I'm not sure what I shall find.' The words were spilling out; she was trying to keep a grip on herself.

Claire knew the feeling. 'Is someone taking you to the station?' she asked anxiously.

'The C.O. has arranged for me to be taken into Norwich. I'll be home by mid-afternoon. Sorry everything is in such a mess.' Edna looked helplessly at the papers scattered over the desk. 'There was a flap on this morning. I haven't finished sorting these yet, and I expect the next lot will start coming through any time now. Do you know how to use the scrambler phone?'

'Of course. Like you, I use it every day. I can cope,' Claire said, watching Edna struggling to remain outwardly cool, knowing that an equally cool approach was the only way to help. 'Let us know how things are.'

Edna nodded and, gathering up her things, she gasped: 'Thanks, Claire,' and bolted for the door.

Claire wanted to run after her, but she knew it would not help, and her job was to cope with the flood of information from Group, to get it to the operations rooms and keep the co-ordination under control.

Altogether it was a bad week for the Oboe operators. With victory becoming less of a dream and more tangible every day there should have been general elation, but it was soured by a series of tragedies.

Towards the end of a fourteen hour stretch of duty, Claire had just finished telephoning last minute adjustments to the morning's raids to each of the operations rooms when her relief came on duty.

'Where's Sally?' Claire said, frowning as Janet came in to take over.

'You haven't heard?'

'Heard what?'

'Her husband has died.'

'I thought he was a prisoner of war,' Claire said.

'He was.' Janet had obviously been crying. 'I don't know the details. But that's not all. Brenda's husband crashed on landing . . .'

Claire bit her thumb hard. 'Not dead?' she said, thinking of the proud little brunette who idolized her fighter-pilot husband.

Janet nodded, closing her eyes in a vain attempt to stop the tears flowing again. 'Her father came to pick her up,' she said. 'I've never seen anyone go to pieces like that. Oh, Claire! It was terrible.'

The telephone rang again. Claire picked it up. More details were coming through. There was obviously going to be little respite that day. Janet took over, but not until there was a lull in the proceedings.

'We'll have to cope on our own. We need to work out some sort of two-watch system for the time being,' Claire said. 'I'll be back here at one.'

'You'll be dead on your feet!'

'We've got no choice. There's no one else who knows the drill.'

Back at the hut everything seemed strangely silent. One of the girls was tidying Brenda's empty bed space, stacking the blankets and putting the locker straight. Claire did the same for Edna, and then organized a call for eleven-thirty.

Her head hardly seemed to hit the pillow before she was being shaken by the shoulder. She went to the bath hut in a daze. Only after lunch did she begin to feel more human.

'I'll be back at six,' Janet said when Claire took over once more. 'Weren't you supposed to be meeting David today?'

Claire nodded. 'He'll understand,' she said. 'There are times when he can't make it either. I'll see him in a day or two.'

But it was nearly three weeks before Claire could get any time off. She and Janet shared the Control Room duties. For the first few days of sleeping one night in two, they felt tired, but the initial weariness was overtaken by a state of disciplined order. Nothing was skimped or overlooked. Being constantly busy helped. There was no time to consider tiredness. For Claire, it just didn't exist.

She wrote to David telling him that she would not be able to get into Norwich for a while. She was unable to elaborate. Any reference to work, no matter how innocent, would have been deleted by the censor.

She wondered if he might think she was stalling again, afraid of the future. When at last she did meet him, the atmosphere was strained.

'Good of you to come,' he said stiffly, only half joking.

'I came as soon as I could.' She was hurt. He was being unreasonable.

'I guess I come pretty low on your list of priorities.'

Her weariness showed in her eyes.

'Claire!' He was suddenly full of concern. 'What have they been doing to you? You look worn out. Can't you get some leave?'

'Not a hope. In fact, I've got to get back by one to go on duty again.'

'Tonight? Zero-one-hundred hours?'

'No.' She glanced at her watch. 'Thirteen hundred this afternoon. I'll have to be on my way. I just . . . wanted to see you.'

'I'll take you back,' he said. 'How are you fixed for the rest of this week — and next?'

She shook her head. 'Sorry David. If there was any way . . . ' She paused, looking forlorn. 'Are you on leave?'

'From today.' He too looked dejected. 'And I had such great ideas.'

'I bet you had.' She chuckled.

'That's better.' He cupped her face in his hands. 'Even if I have to win this war single-handed, we're going to have some time to ourselves . . . and soon.'

He drove her back to Summerton, reluctant to let her go at the camp gates.

'If you really can't get away for the next couple of weeks, would you object if I took up your grandmother's invitation?'

'Of course not. How I wish I could go with you. Next time perhaps.'

The proximity of the Guard Room made it too public a place for any fond farewell. They kissed briefly.

With a heavy heart Claire watched him drive away.

13

The next letter from her grandmother told Claire a great deal more than was written on the two closely packed pages; she began to feel almost glad that David had gone on his own and had managed to get to know the two women so well.

'. . . and although I was well and truly beaten at chess, the vicar got the better of him,' Mrs Grant had written, and Claire could almost see the twinkle in her grandmother's eyes.

'We were worried about young Ivor,' the letter continued, 'because he very much resented another man on the scene. However, after half a day, there was no parting them. Blodwen considers David a true son — or grandson — of Wales. As such, he can do no wrong in her eyes.'

Claire read and re-read the letter, the warm feeling from the pages coming out to cheer her.

She lay back on her bed and was almost asleep when the door of her room opened and Edna came in.

'You're back?' Claire raised herself on one elbow.

'Mum insisted.'

'She's not too badly hurt then?'

'No. She was lucky. Concussion and some very nasty cuts.'

'You call that lucky?'

'It could have been a lot worse. She's home again, and she wouldn't hear of me applying for an extension of leave. She's got good neighbours, and my kid sister does the shopping.'

'What a relief! I was worried for you.'

'You look tired, Claire. Too many late nights?'

'You could say that.' Claire stifled a yawn. 'We've been on a two-watch system in the Control Room.'

'When did you come off duty?'

'Eight. On again at one.'

'Not on your life!' Edna said firmly. 'You're on a three watch as from now. I'll go on at one today.'

Claire slept until late afternoon when one of the girls in the hut looked in with a mug of tea.

'The 'passion wagon' is going into Norwich tonight. D'you want a place on it?'

Claire collected her thoughts and said, 'Yes, please . . . if I can get a late pass.'

Signing the pass, the WAAF officer said, 'You look as though you'd be better in bed, Corporal. But you've had little enough relaxation lately, perhaps a few hours out of camp may do you more good.'

In Norwich, Claire went straight to the hotel where she and David usually met, but without much hope of seeing him. Two other girls from the hut were going there to dinner. She ate with them, and they were having coffee in the lounge afterwards when a voice said, 'You're Dave Powell's girl, aren't you?' It was one of the officers she had seen with David on previous occasions.

'Yes,' she said hesitantly, unwilling yet to allow their relationship to be public property.

'He's around somewhere. Comes in and out of here like a Yo-Yo. You sit tight. I'll find him.'

Claire's friends decided to go on to a dance. She was sitting alone almost giving up hope of seeing David when there was a rush of footsteps from the foyer.

'Hello stranger.' His voice was warm, sending a shiver of joy through her. 'Long time, no see.'

'Too long,' she said. 'Did you enjoy your leave?'

'I had a terrific time. I've been writing to my folk back home telling them about it.'

He sat beside her. 'I was just about to go back to base when Spike found me.'

182

He took her hands in his. 'But, Claire,' he added sternly, 'when are *you* going to take some leave? You can't go on like this much longer.'

'Things are getting easier,' she said. 'With a bit of luck, I think I might get a forty-eight hour pass next week.'

'No hope of getting home?'

'Not yet.'

'If you could make Wednesday . . . there's a small hotel Spike has been to . . . '

'Spike?'

'He spoke to you earlier.'

'What have you in mind?' Her tone was guarded.

'A table for two . . . '

'That's not what I meant,' she interrupted, 'and you know it.'

'Oh!' His face had a look of injured innocence. 'Separate rooms . . . of course.'

'So long as that's understood.'

The innocence was replaced by a wicked grin. 'I don't want you to take off like a scalded cat!'

Claire got her forty-eight hour pass, and three days later they met again, this time at the bus terminus.

'We'll leave your grip at the hotel,' David said, taking the holdall from her hand and leading her past the endless bus queues, through the unfamiliar narrow streets to the small private hotel.

The proprietor showed them their rooms. Claire had a sunny room overlooking a square courtyard at the back, and David had the adjacent room at the front.

'We'll be in for dinner,' David told the proprietor as they went out again.

They walked first to the castle, lingering to view the pictures in the art gallery. Later they wandered down to the cathedral with its Norman tower and slender spire. Claire had been in the cathedral many times, but she thrilled to David's enthusiasm as he pointed out the slender columns and rounded arches reaching up to the tracery of the vaulting; the finely carved choir stalls with their quaint misericords; the cloister bosses of infinite variety. She saw it all with new eyes. She saw too that life with David would be rich, her horizons would expand with his.

After tea, a habit which David had acquired from Blodwen, they explored the narrow side streets of the city with its maze of little shops and houses.

'Oh, look!' Claire exclaimed, pausing outside a drapery which also sold stuffed toys. 'I had a bear like that once.' She pointed to a small fawn-coloured teddy bear propped against the corner of the window.

'He was blown up in the blitz. Poor old Puffy.'

'Puffy? What a name for a bear!'

'He never had much of a growl; just a sort of sigh.' But Claire found she was talking to herself. David was inside the shop, and a hand reached into the window to remove the bear.

'He's a sorry looking fellow,' he said, coming out a few moments later and handing her the faded toy. 'Puffy Mark II. Can you give him a good home?'

Claire smoothed the rumpled fur. 'Thank you, David.' She smiled, but she was near to tears. 'A lovely thought. He's a link with my past.'

'And our future.'

She nodded. 'Our mascot. I'll cherish him.'

'We've still got plenty of time before dinner,' David said. 'You look as though you've had enough walking for one day. If the queues are not too long, how about taking in a movie?'

Claire agreed. She was glad to sit down. In the back row of the stalls she fell asleep with her head on David's shoulder.

'Come on, sleepyhead,' he whispered when the show was over. 'You don't want to sleep through that lot again, do you?'

Startled, she opened her eyes. 'I must have dropped off,' she said apologetically, blinking as the lights went up.

At the hotel there was a message waiting for David.

'I'm sorry, Claire,' he said. 'I'll have to get back first thing in the morning. It seems we can't even get two days together.'

They lingered over dinner.

'What will you do after the war?' Claire said.

'Spend as much time as I can with you.'

'For a living.'

'Go back to the advertising agency, I guess.' He paused. 'And, if I'm good enough, I want to paint.'

'When you told me about the studio I thought it was just a hobby.'

'So it was, but I've always hoped that one day it might become something more than that.'

The hotel proprietor looked in on them once or twice, finally asking, 'Would you be wanting anything else, sir?'

David looked at Claire. She shook her head.

'No thank you,' he said, and as an afterthought, 'Say! Are we keeping you up?'

The man looked embarrassed. 'Well, we've had several disturbed nights lately, with the flying bombs and that. And what with the wife expecting any minute now . . . '

Claire and David got up from the table at the same time.

'I don't want to rush you,' the proprietor said with growing confusion. 'If you wouldn't mind putting out the lights, there's a fire on in the small lounge, and plenty of logs in the basket. You're welcome to stay down as long as you like.'

'Thanks,' David said. 'I'll have to leave soon after six in the morning. I've got to get back to my unit earlier than I expected. Any chance of a cup of coffee before I go?'

'Cook comes in early. We'll make sure you have a good breakfast.'

'I'd like to pay our check now,' David said.

'Not mine,' Claire said firmly. 'I'm paying my own share.'

David turned, frowning, but seeing Claire's determination he could do little but grin and capitulate. 'You win,' he said. 'I guess I know where you got that stubborn streak.'

'If you'll come to the desk, sir, I can let you have your bill.'

When the man had locked the front door and gone to bed, they sat on the thick rug, gazing into the glowing embers of the dying fire.

'It reminds me of the cottage,' Claire said. 'That big fireplace . . .'

'But no rocking chair,' David said.

The heat was making Claire drowsy. She closed her eyes, resting her head in the hollow of David's shoulder.

'Ever get the feeling you're superfluous?' he said with warm irony. 'You slept through the film, and now you're at it again. A guy could get an inferiority complex.'

'An inferiority complex! You?' she said drowsily. 'Not in a thousand years.' She half turned in his arms.

With slow deliberation, he kissed her lips: no searing passion, but something that tore at her very roots. She pushed him away, knowing that this was the man she wanted to marry; knowing it, and yet wondering all the time if the danger in which they lived was putting a false edge on life. Would David feel the same when the time came for him to return home? And would she be willing to tear herself away from her grandmother and Blodwen, perhaps never to see them again? Questions, always questions. Never any answers.

She moved as though to get up, but he held her closer.

'Stay a while,' he said, his lips brushing against her hair.

'Are you flying tomorrow?' she asked, turning her face up to his.

'Could be.'

'Then, you're not going back tired. That's the way . . . accidents happen. David, don't tempt fate.'

She got to her feet and, putting the fireguard in front of the last flickering remnants of the glowing logs, she turned back to switch off the table lamps, leaving only the light on the staircase.

They climbed the stairs, Claire walking ahead, afraid of her own emotions, pausing with her hand on the latch of her bedroom door.

'Goodnight, David.'

Holding her shoulders he kissed the curve of her neck and would have taken her in his arms once more had she not slipped the catch, said another swift 'Goodnight,' and closed the door behind her. She leaned against it, her heart thumping until she felt sure he must hear the beat, even through the barrier which separated them.

She was suddenly very tired. The easing of the pressure now that Edna had returned should have made her feel more rested, but it seemed to have had the opposite effect. All the time the pressure was on she had managed to keep going. Now, after a relaxing day off, she felt almost too weary to undress. Once in bed, however, she quickly fell into a deep sleep, hardly stirring when the air raid siren sounded, and failing to hear the approach of the flying bomb which dropped on the row of houses behind the hotel. She awoke in terror, trapped beneath a tangle of wood and plaster, believing herself to be back in the wreckage of her old home.

'Claire!' David struggled with the door which now hung crazily on one hinge. 'Claire!'

Her room had caught the main force of the blast. He forced his way through the debris and removed the torn woodwork and plaster which was pinning her down.

'Nothing broken?' he asked, feeling her limbs.

'I . . . I don't think so.'

The proprietor was on the landing.

'It's the wife,' he said frantically, pulling on his clothes. 'The baby's on the way.'

David carried Claire into his room which was relatively undamaged, except for the shattered windows.

The Air Raid Warden was outside. He knocked at the door and shouted, 'Everything all right here?'

David put his head out and called, 'There's

a baby eager to be born. Can you get some help?'

'Ambulance at the end of the street,' the man called. 'We'll be right up.'

The proprietor went down to let them in.

'Is there anything we can do?' Claire said, coming to the head of the stairs.

'You could keep an eye on this place until I get back,' the proprietor said.

'Anything else?' David asked the Warden.

'No, thank you, sir. Everything under control out there. A bloody mess, I can tell you. That devil Hitler! I hate his VI's. Is the young lady all right?'

Claire was holding on to the balusters. Her arm felt warm and sticky. In the torchlight she could see the blood oozing from a gash above her elbow.

'I'll take care of that,' David said. 'You get on.'

A cry from the woman on the stretcher told them there was no time to waste.

'I'll go with the wife to hospital,' the proprietor said. 'Here! You'd better have this candle. There are more in the cupboard on the landing.' With the candle, he handed David a bottle, adding, 'Call it medicinal.'

'Thank you,' David said. 'Good luck!'

He turned to Claire. 'Now, let me look at your arm.'

Back in his room, he put the candle on the bedside table and lifted her arm to the flickering light.

'Are you good at first aid too?' she asked, tongue in cheek.

'Cut the wisecracks,' he said. 'I've had to deal with worse than this in the last few months.'

She let him clean the wound. It was clear from the confidence he showed that he was no stranger to the procedure.

'There's a field dressing in my respirator case,' she said. 'It was somewhere behind the door.'

David found the respirator and taking the dressing out he bound the cut. Only then did they both notice that Puffy Mark II was clutched in her other hand.

'He's a survivor,' Claire said with a weak laugh.

'Now, take a swig of this,' David said, holding the bottle to Claire's lips. 'No glasses I'm afraid. Come on, drink up.'

She took a gulp, gasping as the spirit caught her throat, and shuddering at the unaccustomed taste she handed it back to him.

David took a mouthful, and they shared the last dregs. Putting the bottle down, he listened. Claire could hear it too. She sat up, shivering as the phut-phut of the VI got closer. Wrapped in each other's arms they followed the sound across the sky until, through torn curtains, they could see the glow from the exhaust coming closer and closer. The unsteady note of the engine seemed every moment to be failing. David covered Claire with his body, determined that she would not be hurt again. The bomb passed overhead, sounding loud enough to be inside the room, but it had gone some distance before it plummeted to earth, and by then Claire and David were lost in each other, making love in a world that acknowledged no tomorrow.

14

The birds were singing when Claire opened her eyes, and for a moment she could not make out where she was. But then she remembered. She remembered it all. In the callous light of a chill September morning she was stunned by the recollection.

David had gone. On the pillow at her side was Puffy Mark II, a little grimy but otherwise none the worse for the hazards of the night.

Claire got out of bed, stepping carefully across the glass-strewn floor. Her own room next door was a shambles. She had put her clothes into the wardrobe which now lay on its side half across the bed. With difficulty she opened the wardrobe door, first grabbing her shoes and slipping them on, and then picking up the tumbled clothes. As she straightened she looked in horror at the shattered houses beyond the courtyard.

Returning to David's room she turned on the cold tap, allowing a little water to trickle into the basin. Her injured arm was stiff. She cleaned herself as best she could, and was dressing slowly and awkwardly when she heard a woman's voice downstairs.

'Anybody there? Coo-ee!'

'Hello,' Claire shouted. 'I think I'm the only one about. The proprietor has taken his wife to hospital.'

'Poor soul!' The footsteps approached up the stairs. 'Was she badly hurt?'

'No. It was the baby.' Claire opened the door wider.

'Yes, I suppose it would have shifted him on a bit.' The owner of the voice, a stout smiling woman, slow and unflustered, edged into the room.

Claire wondered how anyone could be so cheerful arriving for work and finding such chaos.

'That dressing needs changing,' the woman said. 'You sit down. There's a first aid kit somewhere.'

Slowly, she plodded onto the landing, and Claire could hear her tutting and muttering as she opened one door after another. She returned a couple of minutes later with bandages and dressings.

'There now!' she said, nodding with satisfaction as she neatly completed the job and helped Claire on with her shirt.

'Thank you. That feels so much better,' Claire said, reaching for her jacket.

There were shouts outside followed by a

crash of masonry which filled the air with grey dust.

'Come on,' Claire said, cramming her things into her holdall. 'Let's get out of this room. No point in giving the rescue people extra work.'

The front door opened as they reached the hall.

'It's a boy! Mother and son doing well.'

'And father too, by the look of it,' the cook said, dusting herself down. 'There! Didn't I say it would be a boy?'

An Air Raid Warden was inspecting the front of the hotel, trying to assess the damage. 'You'd better get out of here until we know whether anything else is coming down,' he said. 'Get yourselves some tea. The mobile canteen is outside.'

The early morning sun only served to highlight the broken windows and the scattered rubble — nothing in comparison with the devastation of the buildings behind the hotel.

Claire dropped her holdall on the ground and gratefully accepted a steaming mug of tea.

'To your son,' she said, raising the mug.

Everyone joined in — the people who had lost their homes, the injured, the helpers who had struggled throughout the night — all forgot their troubles in the celebration of the new arrival.

The hotel was pronounced reasonably safe and back at the reception desk the proprietor began to take stock of the situation.

'I can't take your money,' he said, when Claire asked for her bill.

But Claire insisted. 'Business as usual,' she said, nodding towards the wielded broom in the hands of the indomitable cook.

The builders had already arrived and were beginning to shore up the back of the hotel when Claire left to catch a bus back to camp. Waiting in the queue she could feel that first nip of autumn. There had been a touch of frost overnight. Even the sun shining from a clear sky failed to banish her shivers.

The bus was packed to the door. Jostled into a seat near the back, Claire closed her eyes. Exhausted, she tried not to think, but was unable to turn her thoughts from the events of the previous night. No entanglements. She should have kept her resolution. What would David think of her now?

The nearest stopping place was some way from the camp gates. The blue sky had clouded over and a thin drizzle was drifting in from the sea. Claire turned up her coat collar. Once through the village there was still the long trail through the camp. When she got to the door of the hut she was dishevelled and wet through.

'Corporal! Didn't I sign a forty-eight hour pass for you?' It was the WAAF officer on a round of inspection.

'A flying bomb rather put paid to that, ma'am.'

'You've been injured?'

'Nothing serious. A cut on my arm, that's all.'

Janet took Claire's holdall from her cramped fingers and sat her on a chair.

'We'll see that she's all right, ma'am,' she said, opening the door to Claire's room and beginning to make her bed.

'Report to the MO in the morning, Corporal,' the officer said as she left.

Even in bed with a hot water bottle and a scalding mug of cocoa Claire could not stop shivering. The girls found extra blankets and, at last, a little warmth began to return to her limbs. She slept until the evening when Janet, with the co-operation of a sympathetic cook, brought food from the cookhouse.

'Eat it while it's hot,' she said. 'You look like a ghost.'

Claire was surprised to find that she was hungry, and she finished the cheese and potato pie and the currant duff with its cloaking yellow custard while Janet squatted in the corner, waiting to hear what had happened to cut short Claire's much needed break.

'There's not much to tell,' Claire said. 'A doodle-bug landed behind the hotel.'

'Hard luck! Is David all right?'

'Yes. His room was at the other side of the building.'

Janet took the empty plates. 'David's friend, Spike, asked me to go to a dance at the Air Base on Saturday. I don't suppose you'll feel like going?'

Claire shook her head. 'My arm's a bit stiff. I'll have to see the MO in the morning, and I'm on duty at one.'

'By the way, we're back on a four watch,' Janet said. 'If the MO allows you to go back on duty you'll be on night bind on Saturday anyway.'

'That settles it then.'

'If I didn't know you better, I'd say you were almost glad not to be going to the dance. Nothing wrong, is there?'

'No.'

But that was not entirely true. Claire had the feeling that David might now despise her. Although the conventions had been relaxed, the war had not changed the general attitude towards easy virtue.

'You're feeling all right?' Janet asked anxiously.

'Of course I am,' Claire snapped.

'Well, don't bite my head off. It's not like you to be so grizzly.'

'I'm sorry,' Claire said shortly. 'I'll be better when I've had some sleep.'

Claire went back on duty the following afternoon, glad of something to keep her mind occupied. Because of the shift system she did not see Janet again until the morning after the dance.

'Busy night?' Janet asked as they walked back from breakfast.

Claire nodded. 'Never stopped,' she said, yawning.

'The dance was great,' Janet said. 'I was with Spike most of the time, but David latched on to me the moment I arrived. He wanted to know how you are. You've certainly made a conquest there.' She paused, waiting for Claire's reaction. 'Well, look more enthusiastic. I could go for him in a big way.'

'Did he say anything else?'

'Like what?'

Claire gave an exaggerated shrug.

'Have you two had a lovers' tiff?' Janet asked in a mock scolding voice, laughing at her friend.

200

'No, we have not,' Claire said, looking straight ahead.

'I was only joking.'

'You've got an odd sense of humour.'

'And you seem to have lost yours.'

They stamped into the hut. Everyone else was on duty. Janet went straight into her room and was closing the door when Claire called to her: 'Janet . . . '

'Yes?'

'I'm sorry. I'm a bit edgy.'

'That's OK.'

Claire opened her mouth to say something . . . a call for help. But she knew it was something that had to be sorted out between herself and David. She wondered how she could face him again.

'There is something else, isn't there, Claire?'

'It can keep . . . never mind.'

★ ★ ★

Monday was Claire's day off. She went to Norwich to do some shopping. Longing to see David and yet at the same time dreading their meeting, she waited for him at their usual rendezvous, but he did not come. She told herself that he must be flying and decided to return to camp. She got back in

201

the early evening just as Janet was getting ready to go on watch.

'Will you be meeting Spike on Wednesday?' Claire asked casually.

'If he's not flying. Any message for David?'

'Tell him I'll probably go into Norwich on Friday afternoon after Pay Parade.'

★ ★ ★

Pay Parade was over and Claire was getting ready to walk into the village to catch the bus when there was an explosion which lifted her off her feet and threw her across the room. Dazed, and conscious of renewed pain in her injured arm, she picked herself up and opened the door to make sure that no one in the hut had been cut by flying glass.

Two of the girls in the middle room were on the floor, bruised but otherwise unhurt.

'Whatever was it?' one of them said, rubbing her head.

'I didn't hear any engine,' Claire said. 'It must have been a V2.'

Each morning for some time they had been able to watch the trails being left by the V2 rockets as they were launched from the other side of the North Sea.

She went outside to see how the rest of the camp had fared. There were no injuries other than minor scratches and bumps. The damage to the living site was superficial, and the technical site had escaped altogether. The sandhill into which the rocket had plunged had taken most of the blast.

Claire's arm was very stiff and tender; the tumble she had taken had not improved it. She had arranged to meet David and, although tempted to use the incident as an excuse, she felt it would be spineless and futile to back out at the last minute.

Norwich was crowded with service men and women, but David was not amongst them. Claire waited until it was time to catch the last bus. Feeling disappointed and strangely home-sick, she returned to Summerton.

She tried to write a letter to David, but found it impossible to put her thoughts into words, particularly as every letter was censored on the camp. Screwing up sheet after sheet of paper, she eventually gave up.

'We're going to the NAAFI,' Janet called, pulling on her cap as she came into Claire's room. 'Whatever's this? A paper chase? Coming?'

Claire pushed the crumpled paper into her locker. 'May as well.'

'Wasn't David there?'

Claire shook her head.

'Well, it's not the end of the world. I'm going in on Thursday to see Spike. I'll take a message to your love.'

But when Thursday came there was no possible message that Claire could send. She had to go herself.

'If you're not meeting Spike too early, I'll come with you,' she said to Janet. 'Just for the afternoon. I'll have to be back for night bind.'

Towards the end of the afternoon they took tea in the hotel lounge. People were coming and going all the time, but there was no sign of either Spike or David.

Claire looked at her watch for the hundredth time. 'I'll have to go soon,' she said. 'D'you think they've been posted?'

'They'd have let us know,' Janet said. 'On op's, I expect. We've been lucky to meet them as often as we have. There's a war on. Didn't you know?'

'If I hear that phrase just once more, I think I'll scream,' Claire said. 'Oh, David! Why don't you come?'

Janet sighed with disappointment. 'I think I'll come back with you. No sense in staying any longer. Spike should have been here by now. No. Hang on!' She got to her feet, waving. 'There he is.'

Spike was standing at the door, scanning the room.

Claire felt her muscles tighten, her breath catch in her throat. It had nothing to do with the expression on Spike's face, for that was blank; it was something in the way his eyes searched without wanting to find. When he caught sight of Janet, and then of her, there was no longer a shadow of doubt in Claire's mind. She knew what he had come to say. She sat very straight, her hands tightly clasped in her lap.

'Hello, Spike,' Janet said, trying to smile, to put him at his ease.

'We can't talk here.' He glanced around the crowded lounge.

'I was just going for the bus anyway,' Claire said, getting up and walking ahead of them. Once outside, she turned back to Spike and said, 'I know what you've come to say. Is there . . . is there any hope?'

He looked down at his shoes. 'Sorry, kid. They saw him go down. He almost made a landing, but the kite went up in flames as it hit the deck.'

A shudder ran through Claire and she closed her eyes briefly, but it was the only sign she gave. 'Thank you for letting me know,' she said, staring into the distance.

He put a hand on her shoulder. 'I'll take you back to camp.'

'Oh, God! It isn't fair!' Janet said quietly, but with a ferocity which made Claire bunch her fists together in an attempt to keep control.

The bumpy ride was accomplished at speed. It was no occasion for idle chat.

'I'll do your watch for you,' Janet said when they arrived at the gates.

'Thanks, Janet, but I'd prefer to work.' Claire jumped down from the jeep. 'And I'd like to be on my own for a while, if you don't mind.'

Spike had got out and was standing beside her. She swallowed hard, trying to find the words to thank him. There was no need. He put his arms around her and held her until, gently, she pushed him away.

Afterwards, Claire remembered nothing of the walk back to the hut, or the cheerful greetings which she ignored as she closed the door of her room. Life had given and stolen once too often. Tucked away in the recesses of her mind there had always been the suppressed fear of this final blow, checked by the belief that fate could never be so cruel. The lesson was difficult to learn. She should have known that war has no rules of fairness; one person sails through unscathed; another is ravaged by every wind of misfortune.

She would have to tell her grandmother of David's death, but not in a letter or on the telephone. She wanted to be there, to comfort the old lady who had taken so many knocks in the two world wars. Blodwen too. The thought of their shock and grief was almost too much for Claire to contemplate. They were expecting her home for her birthday. Maybe she'd feel able to face it by then.

In the weeks that followed, Claire worked every hour she could, dropping her place in the queue for leave, not knowing whether to be devastated or jubilant in the increasing certainty that she was carrying David's child.

'Claire, you've got to take some leave soon,' Janet insisted. 'You look dead on your feet. And isn't it your twenty-first this month?'

'Oh, what a celebration!' Claire said bitterly. 'And yet . . . ' Her face screwed up with misery, and she began to cry softly.

'Claire . . . ' Janet looked on helplessly.

'Perhaps I have got something to celebrate.'

Edna joined them. 'What's all this about a celebration?' she asked, glancing from Claire to Janet, and back again to Claire.

'I'm pregnant,' Claire said, closing her

mouth into a thin line, waiting for their reaction.

'I did wonder . . . ' Janet began.

'And you were right,' Claire said. 'Are you shocked?'

'Surprised.' It was Edna who answered. She looked distressed. 'You, of all people.'

'Are you absolutely sure?' Janet said.

'Yes. I'll be out of the WAAF by Christmas.'

There was a long silence before Edna spoke again, and then she said, 'Put your feet up.'

Claire's mouth opened in surprise.

'Quite right. You've been overdoing it lately,' Janet agreed. 'You've got to take care from now on.'

Their compassion affected Claire more than any form of censure might have done, and it was painful to her to know that soon they would no longer be a part of her life. Once she was out of the WAAF it was unlikely that she would ever see them again.

15

Claire's twenty-first came and went without any leave: partly by her own choice, and partly because of her forthcoming discharge from the WAAF. Her grandmother had grown accustomed to the uncertainties of Service life and, although disappointed, was not unduly worried. However, her latest letter expressed the hope that Claire might be home for Christmas.

Claire wished that she had been able to take a forty-eight when she had heard of David's death. It had been a mistake to keep the news to herself. Each day that passed made the telling seem more impossible. Now there would be the added shock of the baby. There was little doubt that her grandmother would take the news of David's death in her usual stoical fashion, but Claire knew that an illegitimate child was likely to be totally unacceptable. Her grandmother's code of conduct, in tune with the majority of her generation, was firm and unbending.

When the day of Claire's departure came the girls tried to make it as painless as possible, but she had a feeling of desolation which nothing could alleviate. No longer in uniform, she dreaded every mile that took her closer to Wales. In her bag she had small Christmas presents for her grandmother and Blodwen, and for Ivor, but she had never felt less like joining in the Christmas celebrations.

The coat which had been bought for her on an officially supervised shopping expedition — the final degradation — had no warmth in it. She stood shivering on the platform at Chester, waiting for the train to take her on the last leg of the journey.

The train was late and the compartment, smelling of dust and stale chip papers, felt as cold as the platform. The strictly enforced blackout made it impossible to see anything. Claire, huddled in the corner seat, counted the stations until, reluctantly, she left the train.

'Welcome home,' Mr Williams said, greeting her at the barrier. 'Your grandmother will be that pleased to see you. But, there! I mustn't delay you.'

Claire tried to look eager to get home. She was glad of the darkness which avoided the need to keep up the charade. Her feet were dragging by the time she reached the gate of the White Cottage.

The front door opened a crack, sending a thin stream of light into the night.

'Is that you, Claire fach?' Blodwen called.

Claire hurried up the path into the house, closing the door behind her, and stood looking at Blodwen for a moment before throwing her arms around her neck and clinging to her.

'There now,' Blodwen said soothingly.

After a few moments she held Claire at arm's length, her face troubled. 'What's wrong, fach?'

'Where's Grandmother?'

'She's in bed, wide awake, waiting for you to arrive.' Blodwen put her head on one side, listening. 'I think she's heard you.'

'Waiting! That's all I do these days.' The protest came from the upper floor. 'Come on up, child.'

It was an order which Claire instinctively obeyed.

Mrs Grant smiled warmly, raising her face to be kissed. 'It's been such a long time,' she said. 'Now, let me look at you.'

That was something Claire wanted to avoid.

'No uniform this time?' Her grandmother's voice held a note of disapproval. 'You've rather lost the gift for buying clothes by the look of that coat. There's no line to it, and it looks as though it's been thrown together by a jobbing gardener.'

'It is rather a mess, isn't it?' Claire agreed lamely. Her mind was on how she could break the news. It would be callous to distress them both so late at night. Another day would make little difference. 'Look, darling . . . I've had a rotten journey, and I'm sure you're ready for some shut-eye.'

'Yes, I think I am. You're home at last, and that's the main thing.'

Claire kissed her grandmother again. 'Goodnight. Sleep well. See you in the morning.'

'There's some hot water for you,' Blodwen called from the door, nursing a large jug. 'My word! You look so tired, fach. I'm going to put a light supper on a tray in your bedroom. You lie in as long as you want in the morning. I don't know what they've been doing to you, I'm sure.' She shook her head, watching as Claire crossed the small landing.

By the time Claire was in bed the light was out in her grandmother's room. It felt strange to be home. She looked around the room at the familiar furnishings, and at the painting she had given to Martin. Was it only a little over a year ago? To Claire, time was not measured in months and years, but in lifetimes. Two lifetimes away.

She was restless and slept fitfully, waking

each time to a feeling of anxiety.

'No breakfast!' Blodwen said, frowning. 'I've never heard of such nonsense! A growing girl like you . . . '

'Oh, Blodwen . . . Blodwen!' Claire's shaky laugh held the essence of despair.

Blodwen stood looking at her, her hands up to her cheeks.

'Claire, fach! So, it wasn't just my stupid imagination,' she said, disinclined to be more explicit. 'Have you told your grandmother yet?'

'No. And is it so obvious?'

'It's not just a thickening around the waist, you know,' Blodwen said. 'A look in the eyes . . . I don't know.' She shook her head. 'Whatever it is, I saw it in you last night.'

'I'll go up and tell her now.'

'No use putting it off.' Blodwen's face was angry now. 'David . . . is he the father?'

Claire nodded.

'Wait until I see him. I'll . . . '

Claire quickly closed the door at the bottom of the stairs. 'He's dead, Blodwen.'

'Oh, no!' Blodwen rocked backwards and forwards on her feet, the agony on her face tearing at Claire.

They stood apart, unable to comfort each other. Claire turned away and, lifting the latch, went slowly up the stairs to knock tentatively at her grandmother's door.

'Come in.' The voice had no warmth. To Claire it was obvious that her grandmother already knew at least part of what she had come to tell.

The old lady sat bolt upright in bed, her hands folded in front of her.

'I'm waiting,' was all she said.

Claire tried to speak. Unable to look her grandmother full in the face, she turned to the window, chewing her finger, trying to keep control, her eyes focussed on the barren garden.

'David, I suppose?' Her grandmother's voice had the bite of vitriol.

Claire was suddenly angry too.

'Yes,' she said, swinging back to face the old lady. 'Yes, David is the father, and I'm glad . . . yes, glad!'

'You don't know what you're saying. To think a grandchild of mine . . . ' The words seemed to choke her. 'You'd better go to your David.'

'Perhaps that is the answer.'

'What are you saying?' Blodwen was at the door, her black eyes blazing.

Blinded with tears, Claire tried to get out of the room.

'Oh, no you don't, fach.' Blodwen's voice softened as she pushed Claire back into the room and closed the door. Then, turning to Mrs Grant, she said, 'The boy is dead.'

There was a long silence before Mrs Grant said, 'I wondered why he had given up writing to me. Such good letters.' There was another long pause before she added, 'When did it happen?'

'Almost three months ago,' Claire said.

'And you didn't let us know?' Her grandmother looked puzzled and hurt.

'I couldn't do it in a letter . . . everyone reading them . . . the censorship. Telephoning would have been inhuman. I realize now that I should have taken a forty-eight, even hitched home for a day, but I wasn't thinking straight. I kept putting it off. Then, when I knew for certain that I was pregnant, I didn't know what to do for the best.'

'Do you want to talk about it?' Mrs Grant took off her spectacles and polished them vigorously.

In a flat voice Claire began from the time David had found her after his first visit to Wales, telling how they had fallen in love, of the night when the flying bomb fell on the hotel, her visit to Norwich when she and Janet met Spike, and the weeks that led up to her final discharge from the WAAF.

Claire had never seen her grandmother so affected by anything.

'Child!' Mrs Grant's eyes were covered with her hand. 'To think you went through all that misery alone, and then came back to such a welcome . . . ' Her voice broke and she battled to continue. 'You deserved better treatment from your grandmother.' She put her hands out to Claire, whose vision was blurred by tears.

A gulping sob in the background took them both by surprise. They had momentarily forgotten that Blodwen was standing at the door.

'I'll just go downstairs,' Blodwen said, sniffing loudly, 'and make . . . '

'A cup of tea,' Mrs Grant and Claire said in unison, smiling through their tears, the unbearable tension broken.

Christmas was a quiet festival that year. Claire went to church with her grandmother feeling, quite wrongly, that probing eyes were concentrating on her. She knew she would have to face up to the gossip. However, the local people took the situation in their stride, which is not to say that no tongues wagged, but their interest was soon diverted.

As the weeks went by, Claire noticed that her grandmother was getting slower in her movements and she could not help speculating on the effect of a new baby in the well-ordered household.

Ivor, philosophical as ever on the matters of life and death, looked always to the future.

'I'm making something for you,' he said to Claire one Saturday morning, unable to keep his secret any longer.

'For me?' Claire said.

'For your baby, when he comes.'

'He?'

'Oh, it can't be a girl!' He looked quite put out at the idea.

'No choice in the matter,' Claire said, laughing.

'When he's born,' Ivor continued stubbornly, 'he'll want somewhere to sleep.'

'Yes . . . .'

'Well, I'm making him a cradle.'

The smile on Claire's face was everything that Ivor could have hoped for.

'You're pleased?' he said.

'Delighted.'

Claire made up her mind that, even if the cradle looked like an old shoe box, her baby would sleep in it.

'I'll bring it along next week. Almost finished it is.'

And when Ivor came the following week he had his handcart in tow. On the cart was a large object wrapped in a white sheet and tied with a blue ribbon.

'Here it is,' he called. 'Auntie Gwyneth says she'll have her sheet back if you don't mind. We didn't want the cradle to get dirty.'

Blodwen came to the door to see what was going on, and she helped Ivor to carry the awkward bundle inside.

'Well, open it,' Ivor said, standing back and looking up at Claire.

She pulled the end of the ribbon bow and the sheet fell away revealing a simple wooden cradle with a bird, its wings spread, carved at one end.

'It's beautiful,' Claire said, almost lost for words. She ran her fingers over the smoothed wood. The cradle moved gently on the carefully shaped rockers. 'So beautifully made. Did you do it all yourself?'

'I had a bit of help,' Ivor admitted. 'But I did most of it. You really like it?'

'I think it's perfect. Do you think we could get it up into my room?'

'Lift that!' Blodwen said angrily. 'Are you mad, woman? If you want it upstairs, I'll give Ivor a hand with it.'

She opened the door onto the narrow staircase.

'Let me go first,' Ivor said. 'I can take the weight if you'll just guide it up and stop it knocking against the wall.'

Mrs Grant appeared on the top landing. 'Whatever is going on?' she said.

'Ivor has made the most beautiful cradle, and he is taking it upstairs,' Claire called over Blodwen's shoulder, climbing the stairs behind her.

Putting it down in the bedroom, Ivor patted the side and it moved slightly in response to his touch, to settle again on its shallow rockers.

'I call that a very handsome present,' Mrs Grant said, bending down to give it closer inspection.

Claire dropped a cushion inside and on top she placed Puffy Mark II. It was the first time she had really visualized a baby in that room. Until that moment, a nebulous happening in the future; now, a child. She could almost hear the whimpering cry.

'Thank you, Ivor,' she said, kissing him soundly on the cheek.

His reaction was mixed: embarrassment and pleasure, with not a little pride.

The arrival of the cradle was the prelude to much activity. Clothing coupons were used to buy soft white wool, and in the evenings the click of knitting needles accompanied the radio, only silenced for the ritual of the nine o'clock news.

Mrs Grant did not knit. She sat with an

open book or a crossword puzzle, unsolved, in her lap. Each evening, as soon as the news was over, she went to bed.

'I think I must have some new spectacles,' she said on the evening in March when it had been announced that the Americans had crossed the Rhine at Remagen. 'Without the wireless I'd be completely out of touch. I can't seem to read the newspapers these days. Wartime ink is so poor.'

'Her sight is going, and that's the truth of it,' Blodwen said when the old lady was in her room, safely out of hearing.

'Even Ivor noticed it when they were playing chess,' Claire agreed. 'It seems to have got much worse lately.'

'She never reads her paper any more. Just sits there, quiet like. It makes my heart grieve.'

The following day Claire made an appointment for her grandmother to have an eye test; although new spectacles were prescribed, little could be done for the failing sight.

Mrs Grant was well aware of her diminishing faculties, and the knowledge made her fractious. Despite her limitations, her brain was unimpaired. In many ways, this made her lot harder to bear. There were times when only Ivor could bring a smile to her lips.

When Ivor was not about, and when Claire and Blodwen were occupied around the house, the portable wireless set became Mrs Grant's constant companion, and woe betide anyone who allowed the batteries to run down.

'The charge doesn't seem to last any time at all,' Claire said, removing the batteries from the back of the set one morning. 'I shall be glad when we can get electricity laid on.'

'I won't be sorry either,' Blodwen said, trimming the wick of the oil lamp in the kitchen.

Already it was more than half way through April. Claire went into the garden to gather some daffodils.

'It's a lovely morning,' she called to Blodwen. 'Perhaps Grandmother may come to the village with me later on.'

Mrs Grant did agree to walk to the village. She and Claire went to the solitary shop which sold everything from firewood to chocolate biscuits — the latter on 'points' and only purchased on rare occasions.

Claire thought her grandmother looked better for the walk, but she began to feel anxious when Mrs Grant slept for the whole of the afternoon. However, when the tea cups rattled on the tray, her grandmother opened her eyes and showed signs of interest.

'That was a lovely sleep,' she said, rearranging the blanket tucked around her knees and picking up the Radio Times and her magnifying glass. 'Now, let me see, what have we on the Home Service this evening?'

'Oh! The batteries! Darling, I quite forgot them.'

Mrs Grant, tutting vigorously, shot Claire a frosty glance. 'Well, that's the end of this evening's entertainment,' she said. But her face relaxed, and she shook her head. 'Dear me! I'm growing into a cantankerous old woman.'

'Yes, darling,' Claire said, kissing the top of her head. 'I'm so sorry. I fully intended to deal with the batteries when we went out this morning.'

'Here's Ivor,' Blodwen said, almost knocked over as the door burst open.

'Did you hear the news?' he asked breathlessly.

'What news?' Blodwen said.

'No more blackout.'

'Not even the dim-out?' Claire asked.

'All finished. Auntie Gwyneth says she's going to have every light in the house on tonight, and all the curtains wide open.'

'It can't be much longer,' Blodwen said.

'The war will soon be over.'

'At least the fighting will stop,' Claire said.

'Same thing,' Ivor said.

Claire felt her grandmother's fingers close around her own, squeezing gently.

They knew it was not the same thing at all.

16

Victory in Europe had come at last and, although Mrs Grant now seldom ventured as far as the church, she was quite determined to get there on Thanksgiving Sunday.

'Obstinate as Mr Jones's donkey, that's what you are,' Blodwen said.

Claire was already at the door. 'I'm going to see if Mr Evans can take you,' she said.

'Evans the taxi?' Blodwen looked surprised. 'Is he back from the war already?'

'Yes. He was in hospital for a long time. He wasn't fit enough to go back to his unit, so they demobbed him early. He told Mr Williams that he was hoping to have his taxi on the road by the beginning of last week.'

'Let me go.' Blodwen reached for her coat. 'You shouldn't be rushing about.'

'Thank you, Blodwen, but there's plenty of time and I could do with the exercise.'

Claire's step was slow, and her heart was heavy.

'Thanksgiving' had a hollow ring. Illogically, she still hoped that David might be in a prison camp somewhere in the heart of Germany, but with every day that passed, her hopes dwindled.

She found Mr Evans leaning over his garden gate and was shocked to see how old he looked. She had been expecting to see a young man. This keystone of the local pre-war rugby team, no picture of the conquering hero now.

'I hear you are in business again, Mr Evans.'

The man nodded.

'Claire Grant,' she said, introducing herself. 'I live at the White Cottage.'

'Ty Gwyn?'

'Yes. Are you free this morning?'

He shook his head. 'I don't work on the Sabbath,' he said firmly.

'I'm sorry,' Claire said. 'I should have realized. It's just that my grandmother is so determined to get to church this morning . . .'

'I'm chapel myself,' he broke in, 'but I'll take the old lady to church. Not for money though.' He shook his head again to emphasize the point. 'And I'll pick her up after the service. You'll be going with her? Yes?' His raised eyebrows challenged her.

Claire chewed her lip.

'We've all got something to be thankful for,' he said without bitterness.

'Yes,' Claire said, but her voice lacked conviction.

When she got back to the cottage her grandmother was pulling on her gloves and, with her umbrella in place of a stick, was preparing to walk to church.

'Sit down,' Claire said. 'Mr Evans will be here in a few minutes.'

'Getting the poor man out on a Sunday!' Her grandmother frowned. 'I wonder he agreed to come.'

'He refuses to take any money,' Claire said. 'He doesn't work on a Sunday, but he is going to chapel and is taking us to church first.'

'How very kind. Are you coming, Blodwen?'

'If it's all the same to you, I'll go to chapel.'

Mrs Grant turned to Claire.

'You'll be coming to the service, of course?'

'Yes.'

'Then, get your hat. The car's at the gate.'

When they reached the church door Claire paused, reluctant to go any further. Her grandmother, holding herself erect despite her frailty, took Claire's arm and with a pressure that spoke of mutual support walked resolutely down the aisle.

'Praise my soul, the King of Heaven . . . '

226

The service had begun. Claire found her thoughts wandering to David, to Martin, her parents, and to her brother, Peter — so young to die.

'O God our help in ages past . . . '

She looked sideways at her grandmother, seeming smaller now, but the unconquerable spirit was there.

'They shall grow not old, as we that are left grow old . . . '

Claire closed her eyes. She would not break down.

' . . . we will remember them.'

Her nails bit into the palms of her hands. She swallowed hard, fighting to keep some semblance of composure.

Heads bowed for the blessing.

' . . . and remain with you always. Amen.'

Claire felt her grandmother's hand on her arm. They did not look at each other as they walked slowly from the pew and, with a few words to the vicar, stood waiting for Mr Evans at the lich-gate.

'Sorry to be so long,' he said when he finally arrived with Blodwen at his side. 'But, with your service starting before ours, and our sermon tending to be longer . . . '

'It is for me to apologize for taking you out of your way,' Mrs Grant insisted. 'I am very grateful to you. I must admit, I feel . . . '

She paused, and for the first time showed some sign of the strain of that morning. 'I feel . . . a little tired.'

She slept on her bed for the whole afternoon. At teatime she came downstairs, but not for long.

'I'm rather weary this evening,' she said when Claire suggested that they might sit in the garden for a while. 'I think I'll have an early night.'

'A good idea, darling,' Claire said. 'I'll bring you up some supper.'

A little later, in the kitchen, Claire was setting the tray.

'I'll carry that up,' Blodwen insisted. 'I'm not risking you falling down those stairs.'

'You do fuss so, Blodwen,' Claire snapped.

'Fuss, is it?' Hurt, Blodwen closed her mouth in a tight line.

Claire put an arm around the ample waist. 'Don't take any notice of me,' she said. 'I don't know what's the matter with me today.'

'Oh . . . Claire, fach!' Blodwen's face showed how much she too had shared the pain of that day.

After supper, Claire sat for a while with her grandmother, talking of times past.

'I am happy to think that my great-grandson will be born into a world which may soon be at peace.'

'You and Ivor!' Claire said. 'You have quite decided that I am to have a son.'

'I think we have.' Mrs Grant smiled. 'And now, child, I think I shall close my eyes.'

'Goodnight, darling.' Claire kissed her grandmother and crept from the room.

Downstairs, Blodwen was tidying the kitchen.

'You look as though you could do with an early night too,' she said, looking up as Claire came into the room.

Neither of them felt much like talking. It had been a strange day — almost like an extra Armistice Day — like every Armistice Day there had ever been, rolled into one. Claire envied those for whom it was a simple Thanksgiving Day — a day of rejoicing.

She went upstairs. Undressing slowly, awkwardly, she was glad to get into bed. The ordeal of the day was over, but memories would not be stilled. So many memories. But it was to David that her thoughts returned as, hour after hour, she heard the clock striking the night away. Only when the dawn had already lightened the sky did she finally drop into sleep.

When she awoke, Blodwen was standing

at the foot of her bed.

Claire rubbed her eyes. 'What's the time? Have I overslept?'

Blodwen did not reply. She continued to stand there quietly, her face as white as her apron.

Claire eased herself up on one elbow and pushing back the covers got out of bed, shuffling her feet into her slippers and pulling on her dressing gown.

Still, Blodwen did not move.

Claire walked out onto the landing and across to her grandmother's room, with Blodwen padding behind her.

'I thought she was sleeping, fach,' she whispered, at Claire's elbow.

Holding the bed-head for support, Claire bent to kiss the cold forehead. All cares smoothed away, Mrs Grant did indeed seem to be sleeping, a slight smile on her face.

Later that morning, when the doctor had been, Claire and Blodwen were sitting in the kitchen waiting for the kettle to boil.

'The first time I've seen someone who died naturally,' Claire said with a certain wonder in her voice. 'I didn't expect her to look so . . . peaceful.'

'It's the way she would have wanted to go,' Blodwen said, pouring the water into the teapot and taking the cups and saucers down from the dresser. 'She worried so about losing her sight.'

'Yes, but she would have conquered that too.'

'She was getting to the end of her fighting days, fach.'

'Oh God! I'm going to miss her so much.' Claire pressed the palms of her hands hard against her cheeks, the tears unchecked.

Blodwen felt the same desolation. Over forty years of her life had been spent with Mrs Grant. Now the pivot of her life had gone. And yet, looking at Claire, she knew that she was still needed — perhaps more now than ever before.

'There now, fach,' she said, getting up and cradling Claire's head in her hands. 'You must think of your baby. Crying like this . . . it won't do him any good . . . not any good at all.'

Drying her tears, Claire smiled despite her grief. 'You too, Blodwen,' she said. 'You too! Him. And what if I have a daughter?'

Blodwen shook her head. 'No, fach,' she said solemnly. 'Not the way you are carrying.'

'Another month and we'll know for certain.'

'Indeed we will,' Blodwen said, pouring the tea.

The day of the funeral was bright and cold, as though winter was reclaiming the reluctant spring. Claire was up early. She felt calm, as though all the tears had now been shed.

'Do you mind if I go for a short walk, Blodwen?' she said. 'I just want to be on my own for a while.'

Blodwen patted her arm. 'But, take care now.'

Claire slung a loose coat around her shoulders. Before she had gone very far she found Ivor at her side. They did not speak. Somehow, she did not resent his company. They walked on, side by side.

At the bridge over the railway line, Claire paused. With her hand on the rail she took the steps one at a time, resting a while at the top, and then continuing slowly down the other side.

'You going to the church this morning?' Ivor asked as they climbed the concrete steps to the sea wall.

'Of course.'

'Auntie Gwyneth said you might be staying at home.'

Claire said nothing, and the boy continued: 'I'm going too. Auntie Gwyneth said I could.'

Claire turned to him, surprised and more than a little concerned, feeling that funerals were no place for the very young.

'I want to go,' he insisted. 'Mrs Grant was my friend, and I want to say Goodbye.'

'She'd have liked that.'

They walked to the end of the sea wall and back again.

'I think we'd better go back now, don't you?' Ivor said, standing on the bottom step of the bridge.

Half way up, Claire stopped suddenly.

'Plenty of time.' Ivor was clearly worried by her quick intake of breath.

'Time enough,' she agreed.

They parted at the cottage gate, and Ivor ran home to change into his new suit, his first long trousers.

Claire went up to her room, checking the suitcase which Blodwen had persuaded her to pack ready for the nursing home.

'Are you ready, fach?' Blodwen called from the bottom of the stairs.

The door to her grandmother's room was closed. Claire looked straight ahead as she crossed the landing and went down to the waiting car.

They closed the front door behind them. Half way down the path Claire's footsteps faltered. That pain again.

233

'You all right?' Blodwen asked anxiously.

Claire nodded and taking a deep breath climbed into the black limousine. As it threaded slowly, almost silently, along the narrow lanes, she wondered how the vicar would feel, performing this last ritual for a relatively new parishioner, but one who had become a much-loved and valued friend. At the door of the church his greeting was gentle but warm; the simple service almost joyful.

Claire was glad that Ivor was there, looking so grown up in his long trousers, singing, 'The King of love my Shepherd is,' at the top of his voice. She felt it would all have had her grandmother's approval. It comforted her.

Out at the graveside — ashes to ashes, dust to dust — the last part of the ceremony was soon over.

Claire's fingers dug into Blodwen's arm as the pain hit her again. Blodwen's eyes flashed an SOS to Gwyneth Williams, who whispered to the vicar and then ran in search of Mr Evans, beckoning to Ivor for help. Without panic, and with no undue haste, Claire was shepherded to the car and driven back to the cottage.

'Is that case packed?' Blodwen said as they opened the front door.

'And I thought I'd managed to hide it so well.'

'So you did, fach. So you did,' Blodwen said in a soothing voice.

'And you know perfectly well that my suitcase is packed. You bullied me into doing it the other day.'

'Well, I was right, wasn't I?'

Claire held onto the back of the chair and gasped, while Mr Evans, standing just inside the door, looked increasingly alarmed.

'Now, don't you fret,' Blodwen said, taking Claire by the arm. 'You've got plenty of time yet.' And with a nod to Mr Evans, who took the suitcase to the car, she followed with Claire as though they had all the time in the world.

Blodwen glanced at her watch. The pains were coming every five minutes. She looked anxiously at the road ahead. 'Soon be there now,' she said with a calmness she did not feel.

'Oh, Blodwen! I'm frightened,' Claire gasped, as another stab of pain shook her frame.

'It's happened before, you know,' Blodwen said in a gently mocking voice.

★ ★ ★

'We weren't expecting you for another month,' the matron said sharply, making

Claire wonder if the woman imagined that this day had been deliberately selected to disorganize the timetable. 'Now, let me see, you are . . . ? Oh . . . yes.' Her eyes narrowed. 'Nurse!' she called.

A middle-aged woman hurried into the room.

'Nurse, take . . . er . . . ' The pause was so exaggerated that, had she been in any state to do so, Claire would have walked out. 'Take *Miss* Grant to room number eight.'

'Thank you,' Claire said coolly, before turning to Blodwen and hugging her. 'Don't go,' she pleaded.

'As if I would. I want to be able to go back to Ivor and tell him that your son has arrived.'

'Come on, my dear,' the nurse said, adding when she was out of earshot of the matron, 'Her bark is worse than her bite. Take no notice.'

Claire felt sure that the baby would be born in minutes, but it was another five hours before she was to hear her son's first cry.

'There's a clever girl,' Blodwen said as she was ushered through the door by a young nurse.

'Only a moment,' the girl said, anxiously glancing down the corridor. 'Matron will be back any time now. If she knows I've let you

236

in, she'll have my guts for garters.'

'I'm only staying a few moments,' Blodwen said. 'And don't worry, Matron doesn't frighten me. I won't give you away.'

The door closed.

'Have you seen him?' Claire asked. 'They only allowed me to hold him for a few minutes, and now they've taken him away.'

'You need a good sleep, fach. He's a lovely boy, and with a good pair of lungs by the sound of it.' She patted Claire's arm. 'I must go now, but I'll be back tomorrow to see you, and your son.'

Claire smiled drowsily. 'My son,' she murmured. 'Now, I must find a name for him.'

17

On the way home ten days later Claire had still made no decision about a name.

'You could call him David,' Blodwen suggested.

'No. There's only one David for me.'

'Matthew, Mark, Luke and John,' Blodwen recited. 'Peter . . . ?' She waited for a reaction.

'No. Not Peter,' Claire said, remembering her brother. 'Not Peter.'

Mr Evans pulled up at the gate.

'There's young Ivor waiting for you,' he said and, poking his head out of the car window he called to the boy, 'Here, Ivor! You take this suitcase and open the front door.'

Ivor looked so much older in long trousers. Recalling with a wave of nostalgia the scruffy urchin who took them under his wing on their first day at the cottage, Claire felt it would take some time to get used to this young man.

'Well? What do you think of him?' she asked, pulling back the shawl and revealing the little face still slightly jaundiced from being premature.

'Small, isn't he?' Ivor said, and laughed. 'Like a little Chinaman.'

'Take no notice,' Blodwen said, seeing Claire's hurt expression. 'They all look much alike at that age.' She chucked the baby underneath the chin. 'Who's a lovely boy, then?' she cooed.

Ivor turned up his nose and groaned, and Claire laughed out loud, her sense of proportion restored.

'What's his name?' Ivor asked, taking another look.

'He hasn't got one yet.'

'No name!' Ivor looked shocked. 'By the look of him, he should be Ah Fong, or Wing Lee.'

'Don't you start that again,' Blodwen said, pretending to box his ears.

The baby was whimpering.

'Let's see what he looks like in the cradle.' Claire elbowed open the door onto the stairs.

Ivor sprung to her aid and, waiting for Blodwen to follow, brought up the rear.

The whimper was now a wail.

Claire's room had the fresh smell of laundry dried in the clear country air.

'You've done the spring cleaning, Blodwen,' she said.

Blodwen smiled, a satisfied, smug smile.

'I had plenty of time. I didn't think you'd notice, with the baby and that.'

'All new for Junior,' Claire said. 'Bless you for that.'

The cradle had been made up ready for the baby, the top sheet and light blanket turned back. Claire laid him on the bed for a moment, removing the shawl, and then put him gently into the cradle. The wailing cries stopped at once, and Ivor's face split into a broad grin.

'He likes it, doesn't he?'

'It looks that way,' Claire agreed, tucking the blanket around the now gurgling bundle.

'You haven't given him a pillow.'

'Better without,' Claire said.

'I like a pillow tucked into my neck,' Ivor protested. 'It keeps the cold air out.'

'There are no cold draughts down there,' Claire said. 'You made sure of that.'

'He's strong already. Look!'

The baby had his hand curled around Ivor's little finger.

'Better call him Samson, then,' Blodwen said.

'Not enough hair,' Ivor said. 'Looks to me as though he's going to be bald.' He bent down to look more closely. 'D'you think he's going to be a carrot-top like his dad?'

Claire had not realized that Ivor connected

her baby with David. Even as she recoiled from the shock she knew how stupid it was to think that he could have remained in ignorance with all the gossip there must have been when she returned home. And it suddenly dawned on her that the bird carved on the cradle was, in fact, an American eagle.

They left the child to sleep and went downstairs.

'There's got to be one name you like,' Ivor said, beginning to go through the alphabet: 'Albert, Basil, Charlie, Donald, Ebenezer . . . '

'Stop! Stop!' Claire cried, clapping her hands over her ears. 'You'll make me more confused than ever.'

'Well, I'll have to go anyway,' he said. 'I promised Jones the farm I'd take down some machinery parts which arrived by train this afternoon.'

He opened the door and, turning back, he called, 'How about Simon? Not a bad name, that.' But he was gone before Claire had a chance to reply.

'Simon . . . Simon . . . ' Claire repeated the name. 'What do you think, Blodwen?'

'Simon David?' She looked tentatively at Claire.

'You're determined to get David in there

somehow, aren't you?'

'You wouldn't blot him out of your life, fach?'

'Oh, no!' Claire smiled vaguely into the distance: a smile full of memories. 'Silly, I know,' she said, 'but, until all the prisoner of war camps were emptied, I always hoped . . . '

'So did we all.'

'You did?' There was surprise in Claire's voice.

'Human nature, fach,'

'It wasn't more than that? A feeling . . . ?'

'Just hope.'

'Are you sure?'

'If he was alive, wouldn't he have been here as soon as those gates were open?'

Claire nodded and turned away.

'And where has it all got us?' she said. 'Is the world a better place?'

Blodwen did not reply at once. Then, going to the cupboard under the stairs, she pulled out some newpapers.

'Look at the pages with the pictures of Belsen, and see if you can ask that question again.'

Claire shuddered. 'How could any nation allow that to happen?' She pushed the paper away.

'Easy for us to say. We've never had to

fear the knock on the door at three o'clock in the morning,' Blodwen said. 'Would you have risked your grandmother's life to make your protest?'

'She would have been the first to protest.'

'Your safety might have made her pause.'

'She would have found a way,' Claire said with conviction.

'I suppose she would, at that,' Blodwen admitted, the tears filling her eyes.

'We talk as though it's all over,' Claire said, 'and yet, we're still at war with Japan.'

'Well, there's something else for you to think about at the moment.' Blodwen went to the foot of the stairs. 'I can hear somebody asking for a bit of attention. Shall I bring him down to you?'

'No, thank you, Blodwen. I'll go up.' But noticing the disappointment on Blodwen's face, Claire added, 'I'll bring him down to you presently.'

'Don't be too long. I've got something to show you.'

Claire ran upstairs and sat on her bed for a moment, peeping into the cradle. From where she sat, out of the corner of her eye she could see the door of her grandmother's room. As she turned her head she almost expected to see the old lady standing there.

The baby was quiet again: awake but not

complaining. Claire got to her feet and walked across the landing, pausing at the half open door. With her hand on the latch she opened the door a few more inches, still hesitating to cross the threshold. The curtains fluttered in the breeze. On the mat beside the bed rested the familiar red velvet slippers, touching the hem of the dressing gown draped across the adjacent armchair. Nothing had been changed. And yet the room was so empty.

She turned away with a sigh and saw Blodwen at the bottom of the stairs silhouetted against the sunlight streaming into the living room. Both retreated without a word.

Half an hour later, with her son fed and changed, Claire carefully manoeuvred the narrow staircase.

'Come along carrot-top,' she said. 'Come and see Blodwen.'

'You'll make me really cross,' Blodwen snapped. 'His name is Simon, and don't you forget it. He'll get teased enough as it is.'

Blodwen took the child from Claire's arms and walked through the kitchen to the back door.

'Where are you off to?' Claire said.

'I told you I had something to show you. Now, what do you think of that?'

'A pram!'

'I hope we did the right thing. A joint present from your grandmother — bless her — and me.'

'Oh, Blodwen! Thank you! Thank you!' She put her arms around Blodwen and kissed her.

'Take care! Don't squash young Simon.'

Claire pulled back the waterproof cover. 'It's all ready to put him in,' she said with delight, running her fingers over the flower-sprigged quilt.

'We did wonder about one of those posh baby carriages.'

'In these lanes?' Claire laughed. 'Oh, no. This will fold up and go on the bus, and it converts into a push-chair for later on.'

'Just what your grandmother said.'

The smile faded on Claire's lips. 'Oh, how I wish she could have seen him,' she said, touching the child's face with her fingertips. 'And how I wish David could have known his son.'

'There now, he's asleep,' Blodwen said, laying Simon in the pram, turning it out of the breeze and putting up the hood to shade the sleeping child.

'Come and sit down,' Claire said. 'I want to talk to you.'

'You sound very serious.'

They strolled across the garden to the seat

under the apple tree.

'Well, fach? What's on your mind?'

Claire frowned, wondering where to begin.

'I can see something is worrying you,' Blodwen said. 'Out with it.'

'You know I want to get the electricity connected as soon as possible, and put in a bathroom and a better kitchen?'

Blodwen nodded.

'There won't be much spare cash when all that is done.'

'Are you trying to tell me to find somewhere else to live?'

'No!' Claire jumped to her feet. 'Blodwen! You don't want to go, do you?' She had never considered until that moment that Blodwen might want to lead a life of her own. Coming so suddenly, the thought was doubly disturbing.

'Sit down. Of course I don't want to go.'

'I wouldn't blame you.'

'And where would I go at my age? No. I've got a much better idea. Down at the shop they need a bit of help three or four mornings a week.'

'You'll still get your monthly cheque,' Claire said. 'It's just that I can't put it up at the moment, and I'm sure a rise is long overdue.'

'I wouldn't take any more,' Blodwen said

firmly. 'But, if you don't mind, I would like to help out at the shop. Give me another interest, it would.'

'All the gossip,' Claire teased.

'That too, of course,' Blodwen admitted with a twinkle in her dark eyes.

'I must find some work too.'

'With a baby to look after!' Blodwen opened her eyes wide with horror. 'Not while I have breath in my body.'

'I could do something at home. Learn to type. There must be something I could do.'

They argued until they were both getting heated, money being a subject that had seldom been mentioned before. Blodwen got her way. At the first opportunity she went into the village shop to make arrangements to do three four-hour sessions a week.

'I'm really looking forward to it,' she said when she and Claire were sitting in the sun, shelling peas. 'Even when I was a tiny child I was always wanting to weigh out the sugar and the butter for my mam's baking days. I used to pretend it was my shop.'

'Playing shop, and standing on your feet for hours serving customers, they're two quite different things. I only hope you won't regret it.'

'Fuss, fuss! We'll be better out of each other's hair, I'm thinking.'

'Can you look after Simon while I nip into town this afternoon?'

'Nothing I'd like better.'

'Then I'll get off directly we've had lunch.'

In the busy market town Claire saw her bank manager and discovered that things would be even tighter than she had suspected. Afterwards, she went around the shops with a list of things they could not obtain in the village, most of which were unobtainable in the town too. Feeling vaguely depressed, she was on her way to the bus stop when she saw a junk shop, its window piled high with attic throw-outs. At once, she remembered the day when she had found the picture for Martin's birthday. It seemed such a long time ago. Not searching for anything in particular, she cast an eye over the tumbled goods.

At the back of the window was an ancient typewriter. On a sudden impulse she went into the shop to ask the price.

'A quid,' said the man in the corner, smoking a smelly pipe.

Claire hesitated.

'Indeed, I'm robbing myself,' he said in his sing-song voice. But seeing her about to leave, he called out, 'OK. Ten bob.'

With one foot outside the door, Claire paused for a moment, and already the man had the typewriter clear of the other junk and was rubbing the dusty keys with his grey handkerchief.

'Does it work?' she asked sceptically.

'Does it work?' He echoed the words as though she had insulted a priceless piece of machinery. Taking a crumpled envelope from his pocket he crammed it into the typewriter and bounced along the keys with one finger.

'I'll take it,' she said. 'Have you anything I can carry it in?'

'You wouldn't like me to deliver it, I suppose?' he said with cutting sarcasm, at the same time conjuring up a cardboard box from the back of the shop.

She took the last ten-shilling note from her purse and, thanking the man, staggered out to the busy street. The typewriter was very much heavier than she had anticipated, but there was one more call to make before catching the bus. She wanted a text book on the mysteries of typing, and this she managed with only moments to spare.

Getting off the bus in the village, she hoped that Ivor might be around to help, but she saw no one on her laborious journey down the lane.

'Well, whatever next?' Blodwen gasped as Claire dumped the cardboard box on the floor and uncovered the typewriter.

'I'm going to learn to type.' Claire sat on the floor, exhausted. 'It was so hot in town,' she said. 'I could do with a drink.'

'Someone upstairs with the same idea,' Blodwen said.

'Neglected already, poor little brute.'

'You should never have carried that great thing,' Blodwen said, shaking her head in disapproval. 'I shouldn't have let you go on your own.'

'Just not safe to be allowed out,' Claire agreed, leaving Blodwen still complaining as she climbed the stairs to attend to her son.

In the evening she began to clean the typewriter of congealed ink, old oil and india-rubber crumbs. Afraid of disconnecting anything vital and so rendering the machine inoperable, she was obliged to take her time.

'I don't know why you bought that dirty old thing,' Blodwen said, clearing away blackened pieces of rag and cotton-wool towards the end of the second evening's work.

'It's not dirty now. I've almost finished,' Claire said with a degree of satisfaction, applying a little oil to the various points and running the carriage back and forth to demonstrate the improvement. A final wipe with a clean piece of rag and the job was done.

Each day she followed the exercises in the manual until she had enough confidence to answer an advertisement in the local paper. She began by typing addresses on envelopes, then typing for small businesses and for individuals. It was not long before she had a regular clientele, and a small but regular income.

By the end of July her fingers were more adept at finding the right keys and her speed was improving each day. Blodwen was enjoying her mornings at the shop, joining more fully in the life of the village and keeping pace with the local gossip in a good-humoured way.

The dropping of the first atomic bomb had the village divided: some feeling that it should never have been used under any circumstances; others feeling that it was the only way to ensure surrender and the release, unharmed, of the prisoners of war.

'I'm sure I don't know how I would feel if someone dear to me was a prisoner out there,' Blodwen said, returning from the village shop where it had been the one topic of conversation.

'They must see now that it is useless to continue,' Claire said. 'But I'm glad it wasn't my decision.'

The third day came. Still no surrender.

And then the second bomb was dropped. Blodwen — even at the shop — listened to each news broadcast until, at last, the surrender was announced.

'Thank God!' she said. 'Two of them, there are, come into the shop for their rations . . . both with husbands out there. Prisoners of war. Two years one of them's been there. The other ever since Singapore. Now, at least they've got a chance of coming home.'

For Claire, VJ Day was a day of mixed feelings: relief that the war had ended at last; happiness for those who would now be reunited; but, for herself, no great joy — only a fervent hope that her son would never know the misery of war.

18

Demobilization was slow, but gradually over the months the men and women returned from the Services, taking up their old jobs, and the day came when Blodwen was no longer needed at the village shop. As it happened, this coincided with an offer to Claire of a part-time job in the nearby market town. At first she was reluctant to mention it for fear of making Blodwen feel the loss of her own job even more. However, Claire realized that it would be a means of ensuring Blodwen's monthly cheque and would give them a little more security. When she finally broached the subject she discovered, to her relief, that Blodwen was delighted.

'High time you got out more,' she said. 'You should be meeting young people.'

'Now don't you start that again,' Claire protested.

'I'm sure I don't know what you mean.'

'Not much!'

'Well, you ought to be meeting people of your own age. You can't shut yourself away forever.'

'Can't you get it into your head that I'm

not seeking a husband now, or at any time in the future.'

Blodwen opened her mouth to speak, but changed her mind. Shaking her head sadly she went into the kichen, closing the door behind her.

Claire felt cross with herself for being so scratchy. She opened the kitchen door.

'I didn't mean to bite,' she said, pulling at the strings of Blodwen's apron. 'But you do rather labour the point.'

'I want to see you happy again, that's all.'

'But I am happy.'

'Happy?'

'Content.'

'Time to be contented when you're getting on, like me. Why, you've got all your life in front of you. Now, tell me about this new job.'

'It's only a small firm,' Claire said. 'The boss was in the army, and he's starting this machine-tool workshop on a shoe string. He can't afford full-time office staff, so I shall be the general dogsbody in the morning, and his wife is going to take over in the afternoon.'

At the mention of the wife, a hint of vexation clouded Blodwen's face. Claire ignored it.

'I'm a stop-gap really,' she went on. 'If the

business expands as he hopes, he'll want a full-time secretary and other staff too. The arrangement suits me very well for the time being.'

Claire enjoyed being in from the start and doing her share to ensure the success of the venture. It grew into a satisfying corner of her life, filling the empty hours. The months sped by almost unnoticed. However, by the time Simon was three years old the firm had expanded to such an extent that she was faced with the choice of increasing her hours and continuing on a full-time basis, or finding something else.

Austerity was very much a part of everyday life; rationing seemed to have become a permanency. The improvements to the house, far from being completed as Claire had hoped, had not even been started. If the good times were just around the corner, they were taking a mighty long time to come into view.

'It's no use, Blodwen,' Claire said at breakfast one morning. 'I've made up my mind. Being without a father is bad enough; I don't want Simon to grow up hardly ever seeing his mother. I'm giving in my notice today. My odd bits of typing will tide us over until something else comes along.'

Blodwen nodded. 'I think you're right,' she

said, getting up from the table and going to the door. 'Was that the gate?'

'The postman,' Claire said.

Opening the door, Blodwen held her hand out for the mail.

'Not another bill, I hope,' she said.

They seldom received letters, and Blodwen always scolded the postman for bringing bills.

'No. A letter by the look of it,' he said with a broad grin.

'Well, that makes a change. Thank you, Dai.' And closing the door she glanced at the envelope. 'It's for you, fach.'

Claire frowned at the unfamiliar writing.

'I suppose it might be from Janet or Edna,' she said, running her finger under the flap. 'I don't recognize the writing, but I haven't heard from either of them for ages.'

She took out the letter and began to read it, glancing again at the envelope.

'What's wrong?' Blodwen asked, seeing Claire's white face.

'Mrs, not Miss. It's a letter to Grandmother from David's mother.'

Blodwen picked up the envelope and looked at the stamp. 'But not from America,' she said, puzzled.

'Mr and Mrs Powell are over here for the Olympic Games, and they are calling here on

Friday. Friday! That's tomorrow.' She tossed the letter across to Blodwen.

' . . . to meet the people who were so kind to our son,' Blodwen read. Then, looking at Simon busy tucking into a boiled egg, she turned back to Claire, her eyebrows raised in query.

'He's going to Tommy's birthday party tomorrow afternoon,' Claire said. 'Perhaps it's just as well.' There was no simple answer. 'If only I knew more about the Powells. David told me that his father was strict, and his mother obviously doted on him. Could I take the risk of ruining their memories of their only son?'

'But Simon is their grandson, after all.'

'They'll be over the worst of the shock of David's death by now. How can it help to stir things up? A fleeting glimpse of a small boy they may never see again. The danger of turning everything sour for them. No. Better leave things as they are.'

All that day, and all through the night, Claire tried to take a detached view of the problem, but when she left for work on Friday morning she was no nearer finding the answer.

In the afternoon Blodwen took Simon to the party.

'I won't be long,' she said to Claire as,

dragged along by the excited child, she went out of the door. 'I've got the tea all ready.'

Claire watched them go, still unsure of the right course to take. She stayed by the window, anxiously waiting, every minute seeming like an hour. Five minutes. Ten minutes. Blodwen returned, hurrying up the path, and a few moments later a car pulled into the side of the road.

Blodwen was watching nervously from the door as Claire went out to greet her visitors.

Mrs Powell, small and elegant with softly curling white hair, looked beyond Claire, expecting to see Mrs Grant. She looked older than Claire had anticipated, remembering her own mother.

'I'm Claire.' She put out her hand, and found it warmly clasped.

'Mrs Grant's granddaughter?'

'Yes.'

'I'm Mary Powell.' She turned to the tall man at her side. 'My husband, John.'

His grey hair still showed traces of auburn, and the strong family likeness was a shock to Claire.

'We've been looking forward to this day,' he said, leaning heavily on his stick and gripping Claire's hand.

They were both looking towards the open door.

'My grandmother died in nineteen forty-five,' Claire explained. 'There was no address on your letter, so I had no way of contacting you.'

Seeing the distress on their faces, she added, 'She was getting old and frail. I still miss her so much . . . but, she wouldn't have taken to being an invalid.'

'Better to go before you lose your zest for life,' Mr Powell said.

Claire, catching the hint of iron in his voice, wondered if he was in pain.

Mrs Powell gripped his arm. 'Don't say that, John,' she pleaded.

'You know how I feel,' he growled.

It was as though a cloud had come over the room. Claire introduced Blodwen, trying to break the growing tension.

A sudden shower meant that tea in the garden was out of the question, and so they sat in the living room making small talk and drinking tea.

'Your cookies are delicious,' Mrs Powell said to Blodwen, desperately trying to lighten the atmosphere, but her attempt was diverted by a knock at the door.

Blodwen opened the door to find Simon outside accompanied by Tommy's mother.

'I'm so sorry,' she said. 'He fell into the fish pond and he was in such a state, I thought it better to bring him home to get cleaned up. Must dash! Bring him back if he feels like coming.' And with that she hurried off, leaving one very muddy child on the doorstep.

'Well!' Mr Powell boomed, turning in his chair. 'I didn't realize you had a family. Didn't even know you were married.' His voice was jovial now. 'And what's your name?' he said, addressing Simon, who was silhouetted against a watery sun.

'I'm Simon.' The child took a few steps into the room before Blodwen had recovered enough to whisk him away.

'Oh my!' Mrs Powell gasped, putting down her cup with a clatter. 'Why! It's David all over again.'

'This . . . on top of everything else!' Mr Powell gripped his knees and, bending forward, fixed a fierce glare on Simon who, already shivering after his ducking, turned down his bottom lip and began to whimper.

'Take him and clean him up,' Claire begged Blodwen, who needed no second bidding.

'Come on, Simon bach,' she said, taking his hand. 'We'll soon have you warm and dry. August!' She sniffed, demonstrating her opinion of the capricious weather.

Claire stood facing the Powells. The very

thing she wanted to avoid had happened, and somehow she would have to explain.

'I didn't know whether to tell you, or not,' she said, looking from one to the other. 'I was awake all last night trying to decide. Every minute since you arrived I've still been wondering.'

Little by little, no easier for the second telling, Claire told them her side of the story, just as she had once told it to her grandmother. When she had finished, Mr Powell gave a grunting cough, which could have meant anything. Mrs Powell was crying softly into an inadequate square of cambric, and Blodwen, who had missed nothing, was ready to do battle with anyone who upset the two people she loved most.

'Believe me,' Claire said, 'I didn't want to ruin your memories of David.'

'Memories!' Mr Powell's voice boomed around the thick walls.

'You see what I've done . . . ' Claire was biting back the tears. 'I'll never forgive myself. Never.' Her voice was quieter now. 'Please, go away. Forget you ever came here. Remember David as you've always remembered him.'

Mrs Powell got to her feet very slowly. 'You think he's dead?' She reached out and took Claire's hands in hers.

It was a few moments before the significance of her words sank in. Claire stood like someone in a trance, her senses numbed.

'You call that living?' Mr Powell stormed. 'And on top of everything, to leave behind a problem like this.' The bitterness in his voice got through to Claire.

'He never knew,' she said, looking straight into the steel-grey eyes.

Mr Powell turned away. Claire could not make out what he was thinking. Her hands were still clasped by Mrs Powell's. She, at least, had not rejected her.

'I . . . I don't understand,' Claire said, trying to make sense of their words. 'David is alive, and yet he never once tried to contact me?' She was thinking of the long hours of the night, of so many nights, when she had wept for him; the struggle she had had to bring up his child. She would have gone through hell to be with him, but he could not lift a pen to tell her that he was safe.

'Alive.' The fact would not penetrate. 'David . . . alive.' Again, with growing incredulity, she repeated the two words: 'David . . . alive.'

Mrs Powell dropped Claire's hands and, putting an arm around her, took her over to the window seat where they sat together.

'He was shot down. You know that, of

course?' she began, her voice trembling. 'The only survivor. He was badly burned.' Her hands twisted the handkerchief, and Claire could see how much it was costing her to recall all the details. 'His limbs were broken; his pelvis crushed. It was a miracle that he didn't die.' A quick laugh escaped her lips. 'The Germans saved his life. Isn't that just too crazy?'

Mr Powell, who had been standing with his back to them gazing fixedly out of the window, turned on his stick and walked stiffly over to his wife.

'Don't, Mary,' he said, putting a hand on her shoulder. 'Don't crucify yourself like this.'

He turned to Claire. 'There was an exchange of badly wounded prisoners,' he said, taking over the story, although it was clear that he too found the telling painful. 'David was sent back to the States. They'd patched him up in Germany. No. Patching him up is no description of the work they put in: one operation after another. But, I guess they thought he was coming home to die.'

Mrs Powell began to sob again, and Blodwen refilled her cup, coaxing her to drink as though she were a child.

'With each operation David seemed to lose something of himself,' Mr Powell went on.

'You mean . . . ' Claire faltered. 'You mean, his mind?'

'Not out of his mind. No. I guess no one could say he was mad. It was just . . . '

'He'd had enough,' Mrs Powell sobbed. 'More than enough for any man to stand.'

'I didn't think my son would crack,' Mr Powell said harshly.

Claire could see that for this proud man any form of compromise was unthinkable. He could have accepted his son's death with sorrow and pride, but the present situation was anathema to him.

'I always thought there was a girl over here somewhere,' Mrs Powell said. 'He hinted as much in a letter once, but later, when he returned home, he would never admit it. Always asked the same question: who would want to saddle themselves with a guy like him . . . all broken up.'

'Poor David. If only I could have been with him. Why didn't he let me know he was alive? It was cruel.' Claire's voice dried in her throat.

'He probably thought you'd forget him — marry someone else,' Mrs Powell said.

'Or perhaps he didn't care as much as I thought he did,' Claire said bleakly.

'You loved him very much?'

'Yes.'

'You've got to come over to the States. John will fix it all, won't you, dear?'

But before Mr Powell had a chance to reply, Claire said, 'Now, wait a minute! I'm not going to foist myself on David. If he had wanted to see me . . . '

'Please!' Mrs Powell cut in. 'You're the only person who can help him now. And when he sees his son . . . '

'Oh no! I'm not using Simon as emotional blackmail. If I come, and I say if, then David must know nothing about Simon. I'm not sure that I should even see him myself. After all, it was his choice. In all that time, all he needed to do was to write me a letter. It's been a long time. A long time.'

'*Please* come,' Mrs Powell said. 'Blodwen, won't you persuade her?'

'I don't know that I will,' Blodwen said. 'A lovely boy he was, but it seems to me he's behaved very strangely. I realize he's suffered cruelly but, knowing all she'd been through, I'd have thought he'd have shown more consideration.'

'You British had a tough time. Mary and I have seen some of the bomb damage. Horrific!' Mr Powell said. 'That could have been his reason for staying out of her life. Allowing her to forget. Not wanting

265

to burden her. It makes more sense to me now.'

'I don't want to make things worse,' Claire said. 'Do you think I should see him?'

He rubbed his chin, looking her straight in the eye, the way she had looked at him not long before. 'I don't say anything good is guaranteed to come out of it, but I'd say it's worth a try, don't you?'

'You'll have to give me time to think it over.'

Mr Powell wrote a telephone number on a piece of paper. 'Call me at that number on Wednesday evening, after six. We leave for the States the following morning.'

'And if I agree to come?'

'I'll make enquiries about reservations right away. I have friends in the aviation world, so I don't think that should present any great problems.'

'You won't tell David about Simon?'

'No. I think it would be a mistake to mention even your name until you are on the spot. You never know what his reaction might be.'

'He's not . . . dangerous?' Claire wondered if they were keeping something from her.

Mr Powell shook his head. 'Only maybe to himself.'

'And now,' Mrs Powell said quietly but

firmly, 'will someone please introduce me to my grandson.'

'He's been sitting on the stairs for the past five minutes,' Blodwen said, opening the door onto the stairs a little wider and beckoning.

For a moment nothing happened, and then a small face framed with damp straight auburn hair poked around the door.

'Well, are you going to come and say hello?' Mrs Powell said, holding her hands out towards the boy.

He looked at her intently, but came no closer.

'Who are you?' he said solemnly.

There was an awkward pause and Mrs Powell looked to Claire for guidance. 'Can I tell him?'

Claire had had no time to prepare herself for such problems, but she knew that her son would have to know the whole truth one day, whatever happened in the immediate future.

Simon, sensing but not understanding the strained atmosphere, ran across the room and held onto his mother's hand.

No deception. For Claire, the decision was made at that moment. Her son would know the truth, even though he might never see his father.

'This is your grandmother,' she said, taking

the child to where Mrs Powell was sitting, a mixture of delight and incredulity on her face.

'It's David all over,' she repeated, and Claire was afraid she might overwhelm the child on a tide of unleashed emotion. But Mrs Powell was no fool. She could see the dangers every bit as clearly as Claire. 'Well, hello Simon,' she said, smiling.

'You're not my grandmother.' He shook his head in a slow determined way. 'My grandmother . . . at the church. I take her flowers.'

'It's your great-grandmother at the church,' Claire said. 'Mrs Powell is your own grandmother.'

He laughed, clapping his hands and dancing around the room. 'Tommy said I hadn't got one. But I have! I have!'

Claire caught him up in her arms. 'Now come and say hello properly.'

'And what are you going to call me?' Mrs Powell said. 'Grandma? I've always wanted to be called Grandma.'

'Grandma,' Simon repeated, trying the word on his tongue. 'Hello, Grandma.' He kissed her solemnly and then turned his attention to Mr Powell, standing in front of his grandfather, not quite sure of himself: the young cub, and the old bear.

Mr Powell hooked his stick over the back of the chair and sat down, patting his knee as he did so. 'Care to come up?' he said, in a please-yourself voice.

Simon continued to regard this strange man with suspicion. 'Have you got a sore leg?' he asked, touching the stick.

'It's what they call arthritis.'

'What's that?'

'Nothing for you to worry about.' Mr Powell ruffled Simon's hair.

'Is this one all right?' Simon said, coming closer and touching the leg which his grandfather had offered as a perch.

'Sure. Try it for size.' He bent and lifted Simon onto his knee. 'OK.?'

Simon nodded. 'Grand . . . father,' he said, smiling as he managed the long word.

Mr Powell cleared his throat and, getting out a large white handkerchief, blew his nose with some exuberance.

'You got a cold, Grandfather?'

'No. I guess not.' Mr Powell put his handkerchief away. 'Say, how would you like to come and visit with us? You'd have to fly, or come by sea.'

'Fly?' Simon's eyes were wide open, his face eager.

Mr Powell nodded. 'In a DC4 maybe.' And hearing Claire's snort of exasperation he looked up, adding, 'OK. So I don't fight fair!'

'You've got to give me time,' Claire said desperately.

'Could you go through the rest of your life wondering if it might have worked out?'

'You make it sound so easy.' Her voice was bitter.

'D'you think I'm so much of a fool?'

Claire turned away, unwilling to witness the pain on his face. She gripped her hands together, trying to think calmly.

'We'll come,' she said at last, looking to Blodwen for support.

'Whatever you think best, fach,' Blodwen said, torn by her own fears and hopes.

Simon jumped down from his grandfather's knee and ran around the living room, his arms outstretched. 'Bwwwmm . . . bwwwmm . . . I'm a . . . ' He paused in mid flight, looking with a questioning frown at his grandfather.

'DC4.'

'I'm a DC4 . . . bwwwmm . . . zzz . . . bwwwmm . . . I'm a DC4.'

Mr Powell looked at his watch. 'I'm afraid we must be going,' he said regretfully. 'We have to get back to Chester to rejoin the tour.'

With difficulty he got to his feet. 'You're

the best thing that's happened to us for a very long time,' he said, resting one hand on her shoulder. 'But don't set your sights too high. I don't want to see you hurt.'

Simon took his hand, and they walked to the door where Blodwen was standing.

'Take care of her,' Mr Powell said softly, glancing back to where Claire and his wife were saying their Goodbyes. 'She could be in for a rough time.'

Blodwen nodded. 'You realize what it could do to her?'

'She's young.'

Blodwen walked outside.

'She lost her parents and young brother in an air raid; her fiancé was killed in a road accident; and then she met David. You know the rest.'

Mr Powell leaned on his stick. 'I'd no idea,' he said, the concern on his face deepening. 'No idea.'

'What are the chances?' Blodwen said.

'I'd say . . . less than fifty-fifty.'

He was about to question Blodwen further when his wife emerged from the porch with Claire close behind.

'It's going to be hard not to tell David about his son,' Mrs Powell said. 'I can't wait to see you all.'

'Please,' Claire said. 'Please . . . don't make it impossible.'

Mr Powell walked back to join them. 'Don't worry, Claire,' he said. 'Mary won't give anything away.' And, turning to his wife, he added stiffly, 'Not a word.'

'Why, John!' she exclaimed. 'You haven't spoken to me like that in years.' And, turning back to Claire, she patted her arm. 'Don't you worry, my dear. I want things to go right just as much as you do.'

'Don't forget to call me on Wednesday evening,' Mr Powell said, grasping Claire's hand and bending to kiss her on the cheek. 'I'll make the reservations for the earliest possible date.'

It was not until the car was out of sight that the full force of the day's events hit Claire. She stood at the gate, supporting Simon, who was still waving excitedly.

'Goodbye Grandma. Goodbye Grand . . . father,' he called, and struggling to get down, ran through the garden his arms spread wide, already crossing the Atlantic in his imagination.

Only partly conscious of what was going on around her, Claire went indoors where Blodwen was clearing away the tea things. She sat in the rocking chair, dazed, feeling that it was all a dream and that any minute she would wake to find that nothing had changed.

'Alive. Never letting me know.'

'But they told you why, fach.'

'That's just their interpretation.'

'They're his parents. They should know, surely?'

'From what they say, there doesn't seem to be much contact between them. I don't know what to think any more. David alive all these years . . . not wanting me. It hurts. Oh, Blodwen! It hurts.' She closed her eyes tightly, but the tears forced their way through, clinging to her lashes. She brushed them away. 'Something inside me wants to dance, to shout out, 'He's alive! He's alive!' But . . . ' She searched Blodwen's face for a glimmer of comfort. 'I'm so afraid. If I lose him this time, there's no way back.'

'I know, fach,' Blodwen said gently, unable to suppress a sigh. 'I know.'

19

Wednesday evening — and Claire's doubts remained.

'Perhaps David is right,' she said, repeating the arguments she had used in her own mind since the afternoon when she had learnt the truth, that David was alive, and that he had made no attempt to contact her. 'If he'd ever loved me, if he wanted me near him, if he needed me, how could he have remained silent for so long?'

'Suffering can take people in different ways. Who knows what is in his mind, fach? You can't leave things as they are.'

'And what will I have left if he won't see me?'

'You'll still have your son, and your home.'

'And you,' Claire said with affection. 'I couldn't have got through these years without you scolding me on my way.'

'I learnt a few things from your grandmother, and I'm telling you now — you've got to go through with it. I wasn't sure at first, but you'll never have another day's peace in your life if you don't try to see him.'

Claire picked up her purse. 'I'll go to the phone by the station.'

'That's more like it,' Blodwen said. 'Have you got plenty of change?'

'Enough,' Claire said, checking her purse. 'I hope it won't take too long to get through.'

When she got to the telephone kiosk she fumbled for the piece of paper with the number on it, still loth to lift the receiver and give fate another chance to trample her underfoot.

'Number please?'

'I want to make a trunk call.' Claire's heart pounded as she waited for the second operator to answer. She gave the number expecting some delay, but she was asked to put the money in the box, and the hotel receptionist was on the line almost at once.

Claire pressed the button and said, 'This is Miss Grant, would you please put me through to Mr Powell.'

The line went dead and then a voice, heard only once before but unmistakable, bellowed in her ear: 'Claire! Is that you?'

'Yes.'

'I've been lucky — got reservations for the 14th.'

'So soon?'

'The sooner the better, for all of us. Don't you agree?'

'Yes.' Panic made her voice rise. 'But I hardly know where to begin.'

'Don't worry about a thing. I was able to pull a few strings. The clerk fixed everything — right from your station: trains; hotels; the flight — everything.' There was a slight pause. 'Are you still there? Hello!'

'Yes, I'm still here. A bit stunned, that's all.'

'That's OK then.'

'Thank you for all you're doing . . . '

'I'm doing it for all of us. Time enough for any thanks if it all works out.'

'I'd hate to let you down. Please, don't expect miracles.'

'Claire, my dear, we gave up expecting miracles way back. But hope. Now, that's something different altogether. Mary's right. I darn near gave that up too. You handed it back to me, to both of us, and I don't intend to let it perish without one hell of a struggle.'

'You're off in the morning?'

'Back home,' he said with a sigh of satisfaction. 'It's great to travel, but I guess there's no place like home . . . even with all of its problems. And Vermont in the fall . . . there's nowhere like it.'

'So I've heard.'

'Mary's in the bathtub. She'll be mad

that she's missed you.'

'Well, all being well, I'll be seeing her very soon. Have a good journey.'

'Thank you. And . . . Claire . . . '

'Yes?'

'Let's wish ourselves Good Luck, huh?'

'Let's do that,' Claire agreed. 'Goodbye.'

'I'll be at the airport to meet you. Until then.'

Claire replaced the receiver and stood for a few moments before pushing open the stiffly-sprung door and walking slowly back to the cottage. She needed to get her second wind. The early departure date was totally unexpected. The Powells were not taking the risk of allowing pause for second thoughts.

She and Blodwen had decided not to say anything in the village about their possible flight across the Atlantic until arrangements had been confirmed. Now there were so many things to do before they could leave. Passport photographs. All the small details. No time to sit and think.

'I'll ask Gwyneth to keep an eye on the house,' Blodwen said, thinking at once of the practical side. 'We'll have to tell them about it now, won't we?'

'Yes. I wonder how Ivor will take it. He hardly seems like a child any longer.'

'Fifteen next month.' Blodwen shook her

head sadly. 'Never really settled after his father came back and remarried. He still spends more time with his Auntie Gwyneth than he does at home.'

'He'll be leaving school soon, I suppose?'

'No. He's staying on for his examinations. Clever lad, he is. He'll get on, you mark my words.' She glanced at the clock. 'I think I'll go and see Gwyneth now. I wouldn't like her to get the news from someone else. It's not too late. If Ivor is there I'll send him along so that you can tell him about it yourself.'

It was something of a miracle that Blodwen had managed to keep the secret for five days, but now she was eager to be gone.

Trying not to smile, Claire went with her to the gate and stayed in the garden, sitting on the seat under the apple tree, making a list of things to be done. She was there when Ivor arrived.

'What's all the mystery?' he asked. 'They said you'd got something to tell me.'

'Sit down, Ivor.'

He sat beside her, his long legs sticking out straight in front of him.

Claire told him of the letter addressed to her grandmother, and of the visit the Powells had made. This was no real news to him, for small whispers had already filtered through the village network. Gradually, she filled in the details. Ivor did not interrupt, but his expression became more and more incredulous as the account progressed. Claire could see her own earlier reaction in his face: joy masked by perplexity; resentment on the brink of anger.

When she had finished, he said, 'When do you go?'

'The 14th.'

'How long will you stay?'

'Until things are resolved, one way or another.'

'Then, you might not come back?' he said, trying to keep his voice casual, but not succeeding very well.

'We'll be back.'

'But, maybe not for long?'

Claire shrugged. 'I don't know. I just don't know. But . . . ' She paused, smiling at him, wanting to wipe away the distress from the young face. 'We won't ever lose touch, good friends like us. We stay friends.'

His face relaxed a little. 'You're sure?' he said.

'If I'm sure of anything in this world, I'm sure of that.'

He was silent for a while, and then he said, 'I don't like to think of David . . . all this time, with no one to talk to. To really talk to.'

Claire turned her face away. This was the nightmare she could not face, the thought that haunted her every waking moment, day and night.

'I'm sorry,' Ivor said. 'Upsetting you. It's stupid I am!'

Ivor was losing his straightforward acceptance of life, something that had kept his feet so solidly on the ground. Now, he wanted to mould life to suit his pattern, and he was finding it painful.

'Not stupid,' Claire said. 'No. Definitely not stupid. Whenever I feel that the dice are loaded against me, I remember you, and Blodwen, and Grandmother, and I know that life — no matter how hard it may seem — still has its compensations.'

'If it doesn't work out right, I'll be out there to talk some sense into him myself,' Ivor said fiercely, getting up to go.

'I'll remember that,' she said, letting him go to the gate alone, knowing that he had to get away before his emotions got the upper hand.

★ ★ ★

The fateful day arrived. With all arrangements completed, Claire closed the front door of the cottage wondering when she would see it again, and in what circumstances. Ivor had taken their luggage to the station and it was he who was to wave them out of sight, running to the end of the platform, waving until the train had wound on around the coast.

Despite Blodwen's misgivings the itinerary organized by Mr Powell worked perfectly, each stage of the journey slotting into the next with deceptive ease. It gave Claire more than a glimpse into the character of David's father. The smooth plan spoke of determination, adroitness, a knowledge of the world and its workings, perhaps even a touch of ruthlessness. Was she, perhaps, being manoeuvred too?

It took every scrap of Claire's resolve to remain cool . . . at least on the surface. She calmed Blodwen who, after take-off, was convinced that they would never return to earth without some calamity.

An over-excited Simon, sleeping and being wildly impatient in turn, made Claire too weary to appreciate the streamlined reception at New York's newly opened International Airport.

When all the formalities were through she saw David's father, tall and distinguished-looking, leaning on his stick, standing alone, waiting to greet them.

'Well, you made it,' he said, kissing Claire

warmly on the cheek.

'I'd say I've still got a long way to go,' she said, and his quick glance told her that he knew she was not talking about distance.

He took Blodwen's hand.

'Very glad I am to be on solid ground,' she said.

'And how's Simon?' Mr Powell asked.

Claire bent to pick up her son, who raised a pale face at the mention of his name.

'Hello, Grandfather,' he said uncertainly. 'I feel sick.'

'Then it's just as well we're staying overnight in Manhattan.'

In a way, his words were welcome. They were all tired after the long journey. However, for Claire it meant another night of waiting, another night of agonizing over the outcome, remembering those tender feelings of love — the passion and the anguish. Another night to wonder, had he ever truly loved her, or was it simply an illusion she had clung onto through the years?

'William is here with the convertible.'

'William?' Claire said, wondering if David had a brother who had never been mentioned before.

'Of course . . . you wouldn't know about Elizabeth and William.'

Claire shook her head. Then, turning

back, she asked anxiously, 'What about the luggage?'

'That's being taken care of,' he said, leading the way, and explaining, 'Mary comes from the South. We were married during the first World War . . . a couple of years before the United States got involved.'

He was lost in thought for a moment, his eyes looking on scenes long past. With a sudden embarrassed clearing of the throat, he continued: 'At that time, Mary's old nurse was very ill, dying in fact. She had a daughter the same age as Mary. They'd known each other all their lives.' He gave a little chuckle. 'Closer than sisters in many ways. But, Elizabeth's mother thought her only daughter was seeing too much of a certain young man. The poor woman was almost demented at the thought of leaving the girl unprotected, and that's why Elizabeth came north with Mary.'

'Poor young man,' Claire said.

'Not so! He was no slouch. That young man won the mother over before she died. He got permission to marry her daughter. Not that he needed it. Elizabeth was all of twenty-five at the time.' He chuckled again. 'He worked his way north, and William's been with us ever since. What we'd have done without him during the past couple of years, I just don't know. On David's bad days, William's the only person he'll allow near him.' He nodded his head in the direction they were walking. 'And there he is now.'

Standing by the waiting car was a tall, elderly Negro with the broadest smile Claire could remember seeing. His eyes were fixed on Simon.

'Now I knows why you say to me, 'William — you keep your big mouth shut.' Yes, Sir!'

'And that still goes. OK.?' Mr Powell's voice had gone a tone harsher.

The two men exchanged glances, and Claire saw that there was perfect understanding between them.

'You can drop us at the hotel and then go on to your brother's place. Pick us up about eleven in the morning,' Mr Powell said and, turning to explain to Claire, added, 'They're a close-knit family. When we cross into New York State, then William goes to visit with his brother. But, if we head south for Carolina . . . ' He threw his hands in the air, his stick adding to the expansive gesture. 'Why, then we just have to make it a good long stay, or William would never get around to seeing all his folks.'

In good humour they drove to the hotel,

which was vast, efficient, and comfortable.

Simon was fretful, but soon settled down to sleep. It was not long before Blodwen, in the adjoining room, was breathing heavily. Only Claire, so anxious about the journey's end, found it impossible to sleep, her mind a jumble of hopes and fears. The following morning she felt a wreck, in no state to cope with a boisterous child on a long drive.

20

As arranged the previous night, William brought the car to the hotel entrance at eleven o'clock. Everyone was ready — but, perhaps, not all eager — to go. They were soon off Manhattan Island, leaving New York City behind, and heading north for Vermont.

William made the journey easy by keeping Simon entertained. They stopped for lunch on the way, and it was not until late afternoon that they drew up to the portico of a white-painted house set against a background of wooded hills on the outskirts of a small township.

'Is David likely to see us arriving?' Claire asked anxiously, glancing up at the windows.

'No,' Mr Powell said. 'He lives in his studio at the end of our land, down by the river.'

'Day and night?'

'Yes.'

'Alone?'

Mr Powell nodded, and Claire felt all her fears concentrating in a knot in her stomach.

286

'Then, until we know how things are likely to go, Simon must be kept away from that part of the property,' she said. 'You do agree?'

'I'm with you all the way,' he said. 'You've given us hope. We'll do nothing to jeopardize that. You've got to be brave. Just don't expect too much all at once. The war has knocked the hell out of him.'

William's face puckered into a frown. 'If he could see his boy, it might bust him out of this . . .'

'Please, William!' Claire felt the pressures closing in on her. 'Please . . . don't force things.'

'But, Miss Claire, he *needs* one mighty shock. We've tried everything else.'

'Then, you don't believe I'll be able to get through to him on my own?'

William's eyes would not meet hers.

'You don't,' she said lamely.

'Miss Claire, it's been a long time,' he said. 'I've seen him so low he could have crawled under the belly of an alligator.' There was despair in his eyes. 'He won't have anyone look at him. No, ma'am!'

Claire recalled Mrs Powell's flinching reaction to her own words, 'badly burned', and shrank from the thought of a face — a man — she would be unable to recognize.

Would she find that the David she had once known and loved so dearly was gone, totally and forever?

Too late to turn back now. The front door was flung wide and Mrs Powell ran out to greet them.

'Welcome, my dear,' she said to Claire. 'And Blodwen too. I can't begin to tell you what this means to me.'

Simon slipped his hand into hers and she took him to meet Elizabeth who was standing at the door, the smile on her face no less warming and full of delight than that of her husband when he had first seen the boy.

Elizabeth was nearly as tall as William, but about twice his girth. Despite her size, she was light on her feet and as gentle as a fawn. She greeted Claire shyly; Blodwen even more so. Claire, watching their reserved acknowledgement of each other, wondered if the sparks of jealousy were about to fly. She need not have worried, their mutual interests quickly surfaced, and Blodwen was soon investigating the wonders of an American kitchen.

Later, Simon was left with Blodwen while David's parents took Claire down to the studio. She was to remain outside until they had broken the news that she had crossed the Atlantic and was waiting to see him.

Outside the door, Claire could hear everything that went on. At first David refused to come out of his room, but sent William to ask his parents to leave him in peace.

Mr Powell was short on patience and determined to see some result from all his conniving. He brushed past William, flinging open the double doors of the studio.

'If you don't want to see me, you might at least have the courtesy to see your mother.'

David was beyond Claire's line of vision. She held her breath, waiting to hear his voice. But it was his father who spoke.

'Claire Grant is with us.' Mr Powell wasted no words.

'Claire!' There was a strangled cry.

'Yes.' Mrs Powell took a step forward. 'Claire is waiting to see you. And Blodwen is up at the house, and . . .'

'Mary!' Her husband's voice held a stern warning.

'Send them back to Wales where they belong. If I'd wanted to see Claire, I'd have sent for her myself.'

Claire shrank back against the wall. It had all been a mistake . . . a terrible mistake. He had never really loved her. A wartime affair. The David she remembered had probably never existed. Unable to bear any more, she ran back to the house and fell into Blodwen's arms.

'There . . . fach!' Blodwen crooned, holding her close. 'You must give him time to get used to the idea.' She gave a snort of disapproval. 'His father should have had more sense. Not very bright to announce it, just like that. I'd have made a better job of it.'

'David was so angry. You should have heard him.' Claire sobbed. 'I must have been a fool to think that he loved me. We should never have come.'

'We all knew it wasn't going to be easy,' Blodwen said. 'He's been through such a lot. Let him sleep on it.'

But a week went by and David was as determined as ever that he would see neither Claire nor Blodwen.

'Why not let him know about Simon . . . let him see the child,' Blodwen said when, late one afternoon, she found Claire sitting alone in her bedroom. 'Why not, fach? It can't make things any worse.'

'And how am I to do that? Say, 'Here, David! This is your son. Where do we go from here?'. Is that the way I'm to contrive things? How do I know what it might do to him? Tip the balance, maybe. Do you think I have no compassion?' Her voice died for a moment, and then she added, 'No pride?'

'Throw pride out of the window. If you won't make a move, then I'm going down to talk some sense into him myself.'

'No!' Claire got up and gripped Blodwen's arms.

'You're hurting me.' Blodwen pulled away. 'I was fond of David.' Her voice dropped until Claire could hardly hear the words. 'I'd like to see him again. You wouldn't deny me that?'

'Perhaps not, but you are not to tell him about Simon.'

'I think you're wrong, but if that's the way you want it, then I won't say a word about the boy.' She turned at the door. 'Come down with me. You don't have to go inside. Just give him another chance to see you. It's all been such a shock to you both, but he's been living in his own little world for a long time . . . ' She dabbed her eyes with her handkerchief. 'Help him. Don't throw away the last shred of hope, fach. Come with me.'

Claire agreed, more to placate Blodwen than with any real hope.

The double doors of the studio were slightly ajar and David was inside painting a fiercely vivid daub. The canvas was splashed with paint, the raw colours fighting for predominance.

Claire's heart gave a lurch to see the man she loved — had loved and grieved over for so long — standing so near. She wanted to see his face, to discover how much remained of the man she remembered.

Blodwen walked straight in. 'I don't think I care for that very much,' she said bluntly, putting her head on one side and screwing up her eyes at the canvas. 'A bit dark in here, isn't it? I thought you artists were always so fussy about the light.'

David's back remained towards Claire. He stiffened.

'Go away, Blodwen,' he said tightly, throwing down his brush.

'And I thought we were such good friends.'

'We were,' he said, his voice unsteady. 'Let's keep it that way. Go back to Wales, and take Claire with you.'

'Don't let her go without seeing you. You'll break her heart. Can't you imagine what it was like for her, after all this time, hearing that you were alive?'

'Alive? Is that what you call it?' He limped across the floor and with great difficulty bent to pick up his brush.

Claire could see Blodwen checking the urge to help him, moving towards the brush, and then standing back again.

'Well, now that you've seen me, what do

you think?' David said savagely. 'It's not a pretty sight, is it?'

His back was still towards Claire.

'I don't know about that,' Blodwen said, 'but there's many a young man had a new face built. You weren't the only one to get burnt, you know.'

'Good old Blodwen! At least I'm saved the usual platitudes.'

'Less of the 'old', if you don't mind.'

'How is she?'

'As well as can be expected; I think that's how I'd put it.' Blodwen's voice was cool. 'Can I come and see you again before we go?'

'Perhaps.'

'And Claire?'

'No!'

'Just one meeting? She's not far away. I could call her.'

'No!' he shouted, hurling the easel across the floor.

William came running into the room. 'Go quickly,' he said, pushing Blodwen out of the door as brushes and paint pots came crashing after them.

When Claire saw William late that evening, she asked, 'How is he?'

William's face looked as though it had forgotten how to smile. 'He's quiet now,' he said. 'It's a mighty long time since anything like that happened.'

'The . . . violence?'

He nodded. 'But now he's quiet as a possum.'

'At least Blodwen tried,' Claire said bleakly. 'And they did talk for a while.'

'We've all tried, Miss Claire. He can't bear for people to see him the way he is, and that's the truth.' Shaking his head sadly he walked away.

Reluctant to dash all hopes, Claire postponed the ultimate decision for another week, but David still refused to see her.

'We're going back to Wales next week,' she told Blodwen when it seemed futile to remain.

'Oh . . . no, fach!'

'Oh yes, Blodwen. You know how it was when you saw David. How could I have imagined that I might succeed when everyone else has failed? It was selfish of me to think I could recapture the past — something that was all in my imagination anyway. He never loved me. He's made it abundantly clear that he doesn't want to see me again. He's right, we should never have come.'

'I believe he loves you still,' Blodwen said. 'He won't admit it, even to himself. There's got to be some way to get through to him. He needs convincing that he's not a 'has-been'. You're the only one who can do it. You can't go without seeing him.'

'I can't take the risk of making things worse than they are now; making it harder for his parents too.'

Blodwen pushed back her shoulders and straightened her spine.

'Your grandmother would not have been beaten.'

Claire bit her lip, acknowledging the challenge in Blodwen's words. She slumped into her chair, every scrap of energy drained from her.

'Grandmother might have known the answer, but I can't be sure what is the right thing to do . . . I don't know . . . I don't know.'

'Use your heart and not your head. There'll never be another chance. Remember that.'

Claire lay all through the night with Blodwen's words drumming in her brain: 'Your grandmother would not have been beaten. Use your heart and not your head. There'll never be another chance.' Over and over again, the words taunted her.

She sat up, propped against the pillows, weighing David's complete rejection against her own longings; the love she felt for the man who had probably never existed outside her own imagination, against his unconcealed hostility. He had chosen how to live his life, and she could have no part in it. He had made that abundantly clear.

The following morning she broke the news of her impending departure with a feeling of failure and despair.

Mr Powell, with little hope of a successful outcome from the start, took it with typical fortitude.

'I warned you not to hope too much,' he said. 'But must you rush back home?'

'Yes, as soon as arrangements can be made. I'm afraid it was all a big mistake. It's been a great strain on us all, and I only hope our visit hasn't done more harm than good.'

'Please, don't go!' Mrs Powell begged.

'Now, Mary! You know we vowed we'd not interfere.'

'But, if they go, what have we left to hope for?'

'I know, honey,' he said softly, putting an arm around her shoulders. 'It wasn't meant to be. We've got to accept that.'

21

Elizabeth, sensing that all was not well, brought coffee to the large family room overlooking the grassy slopes which went down to the river. The Powells and Claire were sitting near the windows, where they could see Simon romping near the house, with Blodwen sitting nearby, her knitting needles working industriously.

'Will we ever see him again?' Mrs Powell sobbed, covering her face with her hands.

'You'll always be welcome at the cottage,' Claire said.

'So far away . . . '

'Mary! Will you stop that,' her husband said irritably, trying to conceal his own shattered hopes. 'When we've had coffee, I'm going to get William to bring round the convertible and I'm taking you out for a while.' He glanced at Claire. 'Care to come along?'

But Claire wasn't listening. She was hearing Blodwen's words of the previous evening: 'Your grandmother would not have been beaten.'.

At that moment Claire decided, no matter

what the result might be, she would have to see David. She would control her own feelings, make it as easy for him as she could. If only for the sake of his parents, there had to be a finality about the outcome; no loose ends.

She could see Blodwen holding up a narrow strip of knitted wool, measuring it against the small teddy bear which Simon was holding. Poor old Puffy was getting a new scarf, and Claire was remembering so clearly that day in Norwich when David had put the bear into her hands.

'Claire, I'm taking Mary out in the convertible. She needs a change of scene. Care to come along?' Mr Powell said again.

But Blodwen was yawning now, the wool slipping from her lap as she settled back in the chair.

'I think I'd better keep an eye on my son,' Claire said, leaning out of the window and calling to Simon who was running down the garden towards the river.

'Blodwen will do that,' Mr Powell said.

'She's asleep.' Claire was already making for the door. 'Simon always goes for water, and he can't swim.'

Simon had had a good start. Claire ran out of the house, down the long lawn and through the trees. Scanning the river bank, she could see no sign of the child.

'Simon! Simon!' she called, crossing an old wooden bridge to the opposite bank.

She tore back the thick undergrowth which masked the water's edge, panic making her clumsy. Losing her footing, she slipped down the bank and fell into the river.

'Simon! Simon! Where are you?' She kept calling his name.

The water was not very deep, but quite deep enough to drown a small boy. Was it already too late? Had Simon been taken from her too?

Her wet clothes clung to her, so that she had to fight every step of the way back across the river. Clawing up the bank she looked towards the house for help.

The Powells and Blodwen had followed her and were half way down the grassy slope. They were waving their arms and appeared to be pointing to the bridge.

From where Claire stood her view was blocked by a large clump of dogwood. Breathless, and fearful of what she might find, she ran back along the river bank, crossing the bridge once more.

She looked to her left and to her right, but there was no sign of movement.

She thrashed through the undergrowth,

going further along the river bank. Hopes of finding her son alive were fading. In desperation she turned from the river to look elsewhere. She had been beyond this point only twice — each time in the hopes of seeing David. What she saw now sent something akin to an electric shock through her body.

Simon was there . . . disappearing into the studio. It was too late to stop him, but relief that he was safe was uppermost in her mind. Relief was followed by a feeling of helplessness. This was not the way she had planned things. Quite the reverse. How would David react? It could all end in disaster.

Approaching the studio she could see Simon beside the easel, a tube of blue paint oozing between his fingers. He was making colourful additions to the canvas, and was discarding the blue in favour of red as she reached the double doors.

'What the . . . ' It was David's voice, exploding in anger.

Claire held her breath.

Simon, now well covered with paint, ignored the outburst.

'Look at my picture,' he said, wiping two red-streaked hands down his cheeks, adding to the blue paint already there.

'Will you get the hell out of here!'
David said, seeing the canvas covered
with variegated paw marks. As he spoke,
he covered the lower part of his face with
one hand — even in his anger, unwilling to
frighten the child with his scarred, mask-like
features.

But Simon had noticed nothing unusual
— at least, not about David's face.

'Have you hurt your leg?' he asked,
pointing to the stick in David's hand,
mindful of his grandfather's affliction.

David slowly allowed his hand to slide
from his face and, still getting no reaction,
he rubbed the side of his leg. 'I guess so,'
he said.

'Does it make you cross?'

'Sometimes.' He was closer to Simon
now. 'You don't come from around here,
do you?'

Simon didn't reply. He was too fascinated
by his own artistic efforts.

David limped to the back of the room,
calling for William.

'William's cleaning the car.'

'You know William?'

'Yes.'

'Tell me . . . who are you?'

'I'm Simon.'

'Well, Simon, I guess I'd better get you

cleaned up,' David said, hanging his stick over the back of the chair beside the easel.

Claire could see him now. For her, nothing had changed.

* * *

Those arms were the arms that had held her close. She loved him still. Every muscle in her body contracted as she held her breath. Her heart must surely have stopped. Returning to Wales would be doubly difficult now.

David sat in the chair and picked up a wad of cotton waste to wipe the small hands.

'Hey!' Simon yelled, pushing his hand behind David and extracting a scruffy-looking bear.

David grabbed his arm.

'Where did you get that?' he demanded.

'It's mine,' Simon said, backing a couple of steps towards the door and stamping his foot angrily at this man who had taken the bear from his hand.

'Yours?' David frowned, looking again at the red hair framing the defiant little face, and then down at the teddy bear. 'What's his name?'

'He's Puffy,' Simon said, wiping his hands on his shorts before reclaiming his property.

Claire watched, afraid to move, waiting for some reaction. David had not seen her. He was looking at Simon as though the universe had just exploded.

'Oh . . . Claire! Claire!' he cried, in an agony of longing.

'Puffy Mark II,' Claire reminded him, coming from the shadows, soaking wet from the river, taking the final step through the doorway with unshed tears making her eyes bright.

It was not the scarred face she would remember, only the grey eyes looking deep into hers.

They stood for a long time, like two people coming out of a dream: a nightmare of almost unendurable length. David automatically put up his hand to cover his face, but Claire pulled it away, caressing the puckered skin with her fingertips.

Throwing down his stick, David took her into his arms.

'Claire! Claire!' he murmured, holding her as though he would never let her go. 'I didn't want you to suffer any more. I wanted to spare you . . . all of this.' He touched his face and glanced down at the discarded stick. 'And, after all . . . ' He looked at Simon who was busy with the paints once more. 'I spared you nothing. Nothing. God! What a farce!'

303

'Not any longer.'

'I can't make up for those lost years.' There was a hint of anger back in his voice. 'What have I got to offer you?'

'All I've ever wanted.'

'You don't expect me to believe that?'

'Believe what you like.' Claire was touchy too. She wanted to shake him, to make him come back to the real world.

He stood back from her. 'You're soaking wet!'

'You've only just noticed?' She laughed. 'I thought Simon had taken a header into the river. But it was I who fell in, looking for him. He was on his way to visit his father.' She turned to look over her shoulder. 'And do you know that your son is ruining another canvas?'

'My son,' he said, but he was still looking at Claire. 'I like the sound of that. No, he didn't ruin the canvas; his father had already done that.' He laughed, a little self-consciously, as though it was an unaccustomed exercise. 'And Blodwen's going to have some job getting that lot off.'

They looked beyond the doorway towards the bridge over the river. Blodwen was beckoning to Simon, holding out her arms to him. From the smile on her face it was clear that she felt that things had taken a turn for the better.

'That's one job she's really going to enjoy,' Claire said.

'She told me that your grandmother died some time ago.'

'Just before Simon was born.'

'I'm sorry. I took to her in a big way.'

'And she to you.' Claire shivered. 'Come with me up to the house, David. I need to change out of these wet clothes . . . and you need to come back from your self-imposed isolation.'

He picked up his stick. 'I'm going to need some help,' he said.

'Aren't we all?' She slipped her arm through his and they walked into the sunshine.

'And how's my pal, Ivor?' David said.

'Growing up. He's quite a young man now. He's kept an eye on us.'

'D'you think he'd come out here?'

'Like a shot!'

'We'll give him the best holiday he's ever had. His father wouldn't object?'

'His father married again. I get the impression that Ivor isn't very welcome at home these days. He certainly doesn't spend much time there.'

'He'd make a great American.'

'Are you serious?'

'You bet!'

'Are you thinking of Ivor's welfare, or are you thinking we may need an intermediary?'

'Both, maybe. Let's be honest, Claire.' There was strength now in his voice, the anger and the bitterness might not have gone entirely, but there were strong hints of the old David she had known. 'It's not going to be easy for either of us.' He glanced towards the house. 'For any of us.'

'You wouldn't send me away again?'

The stick fell from his hand as he took her in his arms. The slow smile tore at her heartstrings.

'Ma is going to be out of her mind with happiness to have a wedding in the family.'

'You haven't asked me yet.'

'Didn't I once say I'd show you Vermont in the fall?' he said, holding her closer, kissing the tears from her face.

For Claire, at last, the war was over.

McLEAN AT THE GOLDEN OWL
George Goodchild

Inspector McLean has resigned from Scotland Yard's CID and has opened an office in Wimpole Street. With the help of his able assistant, Tiny, he solves many crimes, including those of kidnapping, murder and poisoning.

KATE WEATHERBY
Anne Goring

Derbyshire, 1849: The Hunter family are the arrogant, powerful masters of Clough Grange. Their feuds are sparked by a generation of guilt, despair and ill-fortune. But their passions are awakened by the arrival of nineteen-year-old Kate Weatherby.

A VENETIAN RECKONING
Donna Leon

When the body of a prominent international lawyer is found in the carriage of an intercity train, Commissario Guido Brunetti begins to dig deeper into the secret lives of the once great and good.

A TASTE FOR DEATH
Peter O'Donnell

Modesty Blaise and Willie Garvin take on impossible odds in the shape of Simon Delicata, the man with a taste for death, and Swordmaster, Wenczel, in a terrifying duel. Finally, in the Sahara desert, the intrepid pair must summon every killing skill to survive.

SEVEN DAYS FROM MIDNIGHT
Rona Randall

In the Comet Theatre, London, seven people have good reason for wanting beautiful Maxine Culver out of the way. Each one has reason to fear her blackmail. But whose shadow is it that lurks in the wings, waiting to silence her once and for all?

QUEEN OF THE ELEPHANTS
Mark Shand

Mark Shand knows about the ways of elephants, but he is no match for the tiny Parbati Barua, the daughter of India's greatest expert on the Asian elephant, the late Prince of Gauripur, who taught her everything. Shand sought out Parbati to take part in a film about the plight of the wild herds today in north-east India.

THE DARKENING LEAF
Caroline Stickland

On storm-tossed Chesil Bank in 1847, the young lovers, Philobeth and Frederick, prevent wreckers mutilating the apparent corpse of a young woman. Discovering she is still alive, Frederick takes her to his grandmother's home. But the rescue is to have violent and far-reaching effects . . .

A WOMAN'S TOUCH
Emma Stirling

When Fenn went to stay on her uncle's farm in Africa, the lovely Helena Starr seemed to resent her — especially when Dr Jason Kemp agreed to Fenn helping in his bush hospital. Though it seemed Jason saw Fenn as little more than a child, her feelings for him were those of a woman.

A DEAD GIVEAWAY
Various Authors

This book offers the perfect opportunity to sample the skills of five of the finest writers of crime fiction — Clare Curzon, Gillian Linscott, Peter Lovesey, Dorothy Simpson and Margaret Yorke.

DOUBLE INDEMNITY — MURDER FOR INSURANCE
Jad Adams

This is a collection of true cases of murderers who insured their victims then killed them — or attempted to. Each tense, compelling account tells a story of cold-blooded plotting and elaborate deception.

THE PEARLS OF COROMANDEL
By Keron Bhattacharya

John Sugden, an ambitious young Oxford graduate, joins the Indian Civil Service in the early 1920s and goes to uphold the British Raj. But he falls in love with a young Hindu girl and finds his loyalties tragically divided.

WHITE HARVEST
Louis Charbonneau

Kathy McNeely, a marine biologist, sets out for Alaska to carry out important research. But when she stumbles upon an illegal ivory poaching operation that is threatening the world's walrus population, she soon realises that she will have to survive more than the harsh elements . . .

TO THE GARDEN ALONE
Eve Ebbett

Widow Frances Morley's short, happy marriage was childless, and in a succession of borders she attempts to build a substitute relationship for the husband and family she does not have. Over all hovers the shadow of the man who terrorized her childhood.

CONTRASTS
Rowan Edwards

Julia had her life beautifully planned — she was building a thriving pottery business as well as sharing her home with her friend Pippa, and having fun owning a goat. But the goat's problems brought the new local vet, Sebastian Trent, into their lives.

MY OLD MAN AND THE SEA
David and Daniel Hays

Some fathers and sons go fishing together. David and Daniel Hays decided to sail a tiny boat seventeen thousand miles to the bottom of the world and back. Together, they weave a story of travel, adventure, and difficult, sometimes terrifying, sailing.

SQUEAKY CLEAN
James Pattinson

An important attribute of a prospective candidate for the United States presidency is not to have any dirt in your background which an eager muckraker can dig up. Senator William S. Gallicauder appeared to fit the bill perfectly. But then a skeleton came rattling out of an English cupboard.

NIGHT MOVES
Alan Scholefield

It was the first case that Macrae and Silver had worked on together. Malcolm Underdown had brutally stabbed to death Edward Craig and had attempted to murder Craig's fiancée, Jane Harrison. He swore he would be back for her. Now, four years later, he has simply walked from the mental hospital. Macrae and Silver must get to him — before he gets to Jane.

GREATEST CAT STORIES
Various Authors

Each story in this collection is chosen to show the cat at its best. James Herriot relates a tale about two of his cats. Stella Whitelaw has written a very funny story about a lion. Other stories provide examples of courageous, clever and lucky cats.

THE HAND OF DEATH
Margaret Yorke

The woman had been raped and murdered. As the police pursue their relentless inquiries, decent, gentle George Fortescue, the typical man-next-door, finds himself accused. While the real killer serenely selects his third victim — and then his fourth . . .

VOW OF FIDELITY
Veronica Black

Sister Joan of the Daughters of Compassion is shocked to discover that three of her former fellow art college students have recently died violently. When another death occurs, Sister Joan realizes that she must pit her wits against a cunning and ruthless killer.

MARY'S CHILD
Irene Carr

Penniless and desperate, Chrissie struggles to support herself as the Victorian years give way to the First World War. Her childhood friends, Ted and Frank, fall hopelessly in love with her. But there is only one man Chrissie loves, and fate and one man bent on revenge are determined to prevent the match . . .